I0780192

JEFFREY K. RANDALL

Seth's Cross

Jeffrey K. Randall

Thank You

I thank God for a praying wife.
Regina, thank you for praying sincerely and continually for me and this book. Your relentless prayers, along with moving work and family schedules around to accommodate my writing schedule, was an act of pure unselfishness. Every husband should be so fortunate, to have a wife, to speak hope when needed, to radiate energy with her words of encouragement, or never let a thought of defeat be considered. I am forever grateful. Love you!

Thanks:

I want to thank my mom for introducing me to Jesus. She took me and my sisters to church faithfully from a very early age. If Dad couldn't drive us, she would walk us the four city blocks of St. Louis to Southside Baptist Church. The greatest legacy any parent can give their child is the introduction to Jesus. The conversations we had on many of those walks impacted my life more than she will ever know. Someday, together we will walk with Jesus. Thanks Mom, love you.

Acknowledgements to:

Dr. Sharon Elliott, my literary agent. I am grateful for her professional guidance, listening heart, and her passion for my story.

Thank you to Marianne Hering and Deborah L. Alten who edited my book. I appreciated their feedback in making sure the story stayed true to the historical timeline and the voices of that day.

To my son Ford, his wife, Heather; son, Noah, and his wife Megan. Thank you for all your support. You all help in so many ways. Love you all.

To Janora, Marthann, and Nadine who raised their hand to offer to read my book before putting it out there. Thank you for your time and commitment.

Endorsement from Chris Goodwin For

Seth's Cross

Having known this author for many years I am excited to hear about this book, *Seth's Cross*. My prayer is that it will be a blessing to believers and bring lost souls to Christ, just as the works of C.S. Lewis in times past.
Pastor Chris Goodwin, St. Louis Missouri

Foreword

When I first met Jeff in 2016, I quickly recognized his passion for sharing the gospel in ways that connect deeply with the heart. Over the years, I've had the privilege of witnessing his faith firsthand—on an unforgettable trip to Israel, through our work together on the church Advisory Board, and in his faithful service at Elevation Church. Jeff's ability to weave profound truths into compelling narratives is a gift, and I'm honored to introduce his latest work, *Seth's Cross*.

As a pastor, I've spent years studying and teaching about God's grace and the transformative power of Jesus' sacrifice on the cross. That's why this book resonates so deeply with me. Jeff has taken one of the most overlooked characters in Scripture—the thief who cried out for mercy beside Jesus—and imagined a rich backstory that brings the gospel message to life in a fresh, captivating way.

Through *Seth's Cross*, you'll journey into the historical and emotional landscape of the time, encountering Seth as a childhood friend of Jesus, a man whose life took a dark turn, and ultimately, someone whose redemption became the epitome of God's boundless grace. Along the way, you'll meet a cast of unforgettable characters—family, friends, and a special young woman—who help shape Seth's story.

What I love most about this book is its heart. At its core, *Seth's Cross* reminds us of a truth we can never hear enough: no matter how far we've wandered or how broken our lives may feel, God's grace is enough. It's a message that speaks to all of us, whether we're encountering Jesus for the first time or seeking a deeper understanding of His love.

This isn't just a story; it's an invitation. An invitation to see yourself in Seth, to embrace the truth that grace is available—even to one's last breath—and to share that hope with others.

Thank you, Jeff, for reminding us of the timeless power of the cross. I pray this book will bless every reader as it has blessed me.

In His grace,
Pastor Daniel
Elevation Church

Prologue

Bang . . .
    Bang . . .
    Bang.
    The soldier relaxes his arm because of the weight of the hammer.
    Oh, please let that be the last one. I can't take any more.
    But he does not stop. He lifts the hammer again, high above his iron helmet and smashes the first nail into my feet. The iron tears my skin away before it cracks through my bones.
    Just breathe. Breathe Seth. It will be over soon.
    I wonder why I tell myself to keep breathing. Wouldn't it be better to end it now? To be done with it?
    Bang . . .
    Bang . . .
    Bang.
    The palm of my hand is turned up, and the guard, having no mercy, pounds a nail through it.
    My arms are stretched out on a cross, which is lying on the ground. I see people—a lot of people—standing around cheering the guards on.
    The crowd shouts, "Crucify him! Crucify him!"
    The guards taunt the man nailed to the cross next to me. "Hey, you! King of the Jews, why don't you save yourself? Come down off your cross!"

Isn't being nailed to a cross enough for them? Please let it stop!

Blood snakes down my arms and legs. It is warm and thick.

I am so thirsty. The sweat and blood flowing down my face catch the corners of my mouth. But the liquid offers no relief.

Another guard throws back the red scarf resting on his shoulders, getting it out of his way to hammer in another nail. He hands the nail over for what I hope is the final pounding. First, ripping the skin, then piercing through the bone, and then landing in the hard wood pressing my other hand tightly to the wood beam.

I think . . . *I hope that was the last nail needed to hold me up on the splintery, cross-shaped beams.*

I gently roll my head to the other side, and I see her. It's Mother, on her knees, at my feet about ten feet away. Her face is buried in her hands. At the sight of her son nailed on a cross, she is crying harder than I have ever seen her cry before. If I could carry all her pain on this cross, I would, but I can't.

I regret causing my mother the sorrow of knowing her son was nothing more than a criminal, a robber, a selfish person.

My pain seemed little compared to the agony Mother was going through. With each sob, her body quivers and shakes uncontrollably.

I am sorry, so sorry. I love you.

I see a woman kneeling next to her. Her arm is draped over my mother's shoulders. Her face is turned toward Mother, as if she is consoling her, helping her through this horrific event.

I cannot tell who she is, but I feel some relief knowing she is there with Mother. She isn't alone now.

The woman lifts her head and looks directly at me. And I recognize her: Mary. With hardly a breath of air left, I mouth the words, "Thank you. Please take care of my mother."

A breeze runs across my face with enough force to push my matted hair away from my eyes. It's easier for me to see several people gathering around my mother and Mary.

They are grieving, hurting for Mary and her son, Jesus.

I know they are not here for me, and they are especially not here for the man lying on the other side of Jesus. That I knew for sure.

Take deep breaths. Try to lie as still as possible.

I hear guards roll up the pulley rig. They attach a rope to the top of my cross. They raise the cross off the ground with me firmly nailed to it. There's not a hint I will fall, but even the slightest movement sends pain racing through my body.

The weight of my body shifts, and every nerve responds to the movement. With my head slumped down, I see the three-foot hole that will hold up the cross, will anchor me to the place where I will take my last breath. The abrupt movement of the lifting and jerking of the wood beams remind me one last time that the only things keeping me from falling to the ground are the long nails driven through my body.

In silence, the guards push the pulley rig two steps forward and let go. A large thud rings through my ears when the upright beam hits the ground three feet down in the hard, dry dirt. Everywhere a nail pierces through my body, there is pain, a pain I haven't experienced before. It's a pain I never thought imaginable, and I wished it on nobody . . . well, maybe on my father.

Part One   Never Enough

Nazareth and Jerusalem, the twenty-eighth year of Herod the Great's rule

Chapter One

Seth

"Ruth, are you okay?" I ask.

For the third time, Ruth winces in pain, holding her stomach. She moans softly with each movement. I have no idea what to do but try to comfort her.

"Let me walk you home."

I pick up her clay marbles and the few I have left, after she beat me far too many times, and put them in our leather pouches.

I like Ruth. She was the first person to talk to me when my family moved to Nazareth. She is someone to play marbles with or spend time with on the Sabbath. Ruth enjoys marbles or wading in the pond, catching crayfish. Most of the other girls want to play only with dolls or learn to sew.

Ruth just turned twelve, like me. Her parents gave her a lot of beautiful, hand-painted marbles. Me? Mother sneaked a handful of new marbles in my leather pouch, then whispered, "Don't tell your father about this gift. This will be our little secret."

Ruth has my same straight, shoulder-length hair. Strands the color of onyx lie flat and limp, but they shine in the sunlight.

We are both the same height, four feet ten inches. I want so much to hit the five-foot mark before she does. But she is slimmer than me because I have more muscles, thanks to

Father's endless chores. I can hold my own when I need to wrestle my way out of things with the other boys. For the most part, the boys shy away from me. Except for one. To me, he has a funny name: Jesus. I tease him about it, and he just teases back saying, "Yes, but people will remember my name."

Ruth was fine when I first came. Now every few weeks she has episodes of pain. It seems to be worse. Her parents have taken her to many doctors in Jerusalem. They even stopped by the temple for prayer, hoping for a miracle—but no one could heal her.

"Seth, you don't have to walk me home," Ruth says. "I can make it by myself. It's getting late, and your father is going to get angry if you don't get home in time to do chores before the sun sets.

Ruth is easy to talk to, and so she knows about my challenges with Father.

I come alongside her, and she leans on my shoulder. "I don't care, Ruth, I want to make sure you get home okay. What's the worst he can do, beat me?"

Ruth's mouth turns into a frown at my dark humor. Still, I walk closely behind her, watching her every step so I can catch her if she falls.

I lead Ruth to her house with grapevines growing on an arched trellis over the door. She says she is feeling a little better. It may or may not be true; I hand her both marble sacks and head home, running.

I sigh with relief when I turn down the lane that leads to the back of my house. The sun is still up, lighting the figure coming out the door, shouting, "Seth, get me my strap! Now!" The sound of Father's voice, when he gets this angry, is like vultures screaming as they fight one another for the last bit of raw meat on a carcass. This whip he desires is a family heirloom, which has been handed down at least three generations. I don't know why the beating is coming. I rarely don't. He doesn't need a great reason, just a body.

I stop and look toward the small stone hut that stands next to the pen where the goats are kept. Hanging on a nail next to the opening of the hut hangs a two-and-a-half-foot-long whip. When it's not called into duty, it hangs on the inside of the hut easily accessible inside the door.

Five straps of leather dangle at the bottom with sharp pieces of animal bones protruding at various places for increased effect. This whip has seen many beatings. The dried blood of three generations stains the leather strap.

"Don't you make me wait another minute!" my father yells.

He is serious. I have seen this mood many times. His eyelids are open so wide it seems his eyeballs might pop out. His hand trembles as he points his stubby finger right at me. The finger and the rest of him are close enough that I can smell the filth. He sprays spit all over my face like an angry camel. The stench of his breath takes mine away.

No, I will not wait.

I hurry toward the hut. It makes little sense why I would want to do that. It's like the smelly goats we raise. When I enter their pen, they run to me, thinking I'm going to play with them. Actually, I'm there to pick one for next week's market. Who in their right mind rushes toward what is about to cause them great pain?

I am in a hurry to get it over with, and he is in a hurry to begin what he calls the "stripes of wisdom." He will say, "I don't want to hurt you. I just want to make you aware of the errors of your ways." Not for a second do I think it's about his wanting to help me. We both know it's just to inflict pain. Pain he once endured, over and over again, inflicted by his father. His father, his father's father.

It's a terrible family trait I intend to stop. I probably won't live long enough to have a family, however. I will either die at the hands of my father, perhaps even today or the life he wants me to live will be the death of me.

I may be only twelve, but I know what Father does. This goat farm and mud hut are nothing more than a sham. Father wants his neighbors to think he's a legitimate herder. He has already made it known that he expects me to follow in his footsteps. And it's not raising goats.

I'm just a few feet away from the hut when I hear Mother screaming as she runs out the back door. I stop.

"Aran! Don't do this to Seth," she yells.

Her sandals fall from her feet; her headscarf drops to her shoulders. A look of pure anguish twists her face.

Seeing her like this is a blow more painful than any stripe from the strap.

"Aran, please don't. He's just a boy . . . our boy. If you have to beat someone, beat me." As Mother closes in on Father, he grabs her right arm and throws her to the ground.

It takes everything I have in me not to run to her and help her up, to rescue her from the man who tossed her to the ground like a sack of flour.

She turns on her side, away from him, burying her face in her hands. Father alternates between laughing and cursing at her.

It's a sight I hope I never see again.

I say, "Father! Stop. It's me you want to punish, not Mother."

"Boy, you'd better hold your tongue. Don't you ever tell me how to treat your mother. Now, I suggest you go get that whip and bring it to me."

I turn back toward the hut, and I notice there is a pitchfork leaning against the side, well within my reach.

Is it an opportunity? If I time it just right, I can grab the pitchfork, spin around, and plunge it right through his heart in one continuous movement. He will never know what happened.

For a split second, I consider the unthinkable. I visualize the three pointy ends of the pitchfork tearing through my father's body like a knife cutting through a block of butter.

An opportunity to stop the generational parenting of pain. This could end it. For me, for Mother.

As if reading my mind, Father shouts. "Seth! If you think you are man enough, why don't you grab the pitchfork and try and stop me? You know you want to. What to do? What to do? Are you a man? Or are you a weak little boy like your mother wants you to be?"

I get it now. He put it there on purpose to see what I would do. It's a test. He wants to see if I am going to be as ruthless as he is.

Father was right. I want to. Without saying a word, I reach up, and with force I pull the whip off the wall, taking the nail with it. In one quick movement, I turn to him and reach toward him, handing him his prized possession.

"Here, take it. Do what you need to do." I yank my robe down off my back, drop to my knees, and place both my hands palms down deep in the mud to help brace the blows that are about to come. I raise my head to see Mother. She is also on her knees, still sobbing, with her face buried in her hands not knowing if I will survive another beating.

"Aran!" Mother pleads. "Isn't it enough? Enough that you are turning our son into a thief, a robber like your father and his father before him. Why do you have to beat him too?"

I can answer Mother's question. Father has to beat me because I can't do enough to please him. I can't do enough to make him forgive me when I mess up. I can't do enough to win his love. I can't do enough—enough of anything— and I never will be able to. So that is my fate at the hands of my father.

Without turning, Father twists at the hips and yells, "It's never enough! Seth can't do enough to deserve the good life I'm going to give him."

Slap! . . . Slap! . . . Slap!

Without even looking at me, his generational instincts take over. I grit my teeth as each blow tears at my flesh.

Chapter Two

Seth

Streaks of light flood through the small cracks in the walls of my room, hitting me in the eyes. The light is so bright it snaps me out of the deepest sleep I've had since the scourging. Every twist and turn I make sends shivers of pain through my body, forcing me to relive the whip hitting my back and tearing my skin open.

This morning is different. I can move without crying. For the first time in days, it doesn't hurt . . . as much. I lay there another minute making sure I am not dreaming.

I pat my face and my arms. Great! It is real. But it's too quiet in the house. I don't hear Mother moving about or preparing meals for the day. Father must already be gone.

Okay, great. I make a plan to get outside. Maybe I will go wading in the pond. No one ever goes there at this time of day. I can still be alone, so I won't have to explain why I move so awkwardly.

Mother is probably at the market getting food for the day, or she might be getting water at the well before the heat of the day sets in. I scan the rooms to make sure I didn't miss her, and I see a plate of rolls with a bowl of butter and a cup filled with fresh milk on a table in the kitchen. Mother always looks out for me, even when she's not here.

After moving to the table, I pull up my favorite stool and grab the cup of milk. I love this old wooden stool because when I sit on this stool, it teeters backward and forward. I imagine being on a large boat bobbing up and down in the water as I travel to a land far from Nazareth.

Father hates the stool. He yells every time he accidentally sits on it and thinks it is falling out from under him.

In slow motion, I play in my mind the memory of Father frantically reaching for help as he thinks he is going to hit the floor. His voice rises an octave higher . . .

I remember that moment, and milk sprays out of my mouth across the table. I laugh so hard that a teardrop slides down my cheek. Once I catch my breath, I realize I haven't laughed like that for a long time. Then it hits me: the last time I laughed like that was when Father took me fishing before we moved to Nazareth.

We had been at our special spot at the Jordan River at our old home in Jericho. Father stood on the riverbank, trying to land a big Mango fish. As he danced side to side, looking for the best spot to bring the fish out of the water, his feet tangled in the line. He fell headfirst right into the river. I was shocked; I didn't know what to do. Father's head popped out of the water. He gasped for air. Raising his left hand above his head holding the fish, he shouted, "I got it! I got it!" He looked victorious, even valiant, as if he had conquered a great army.

Father stood in the water, waist-high, and shouted for me to come help with the slippery conquest. I ran to the edge of the bank as he reached his empty hand toward me, seeking help getting out of the river. I leaned forward. Our hands met and I tugged on him as much as a ten-year-old boy could, when suddenly he slipped in the mud and fell backward into the water.

Fearing to let go, I leaned forward to the point of no return. Headfirst, I hit the water just like Father had done. After taking in a gulp or two of water, I saw sunlight.

I was lying against Father's chest, held securely in his arms. I looked up at him, and he looked at me in a way I had never seen before. Without a word spoken, he burst out laughing. Then I laughed as well. He tossed me up over his head several times as we both laughed until the river water on our faces turned to tears of joy.

As the memory fades, the tears of laughter turn to tears of sadness. The number of tears makes the number of scars on my back seem small in comparison.

Chapter Three

Naomi

I say to the vendor, "I'll take six apples, two pomegranates, and five dates." A whiff of sweet apple comes my way as she selects my fruit with hands covered in leathery brown skin.

I hope she hurries. I need to get back home. Seth will probably be up soon. I reach for the sack of fruit the little old lady hands me. The many years under the harsh sun in the marketplace have taken no pity on her. She's most likely ten to fifteen years younger than she looks.

I say thank you as I quickly turn away from the table. But I run straight into a woman juggling three bags of food. All three bags are knocked to the ground.

I see apples roll in one direction, lemons in another. A small melon rolls between my feet. Since the market is bursting with shoppers, the woman's fruits are being kicked around like a child's ball in an open field.

I shout above the vendors hocking their wares, "I am so sorry! I'll get them!" I drop my sack of food on the ground and begin grabbing as much as I can before the woman's food is kicked, picked, or stampeded on any further. I feel as if I'm playing a game of jacks.

Moving around on my knees and grabbing in all directions, I scurry around like a mouse. Several people narrowly miss falling over me. After I capture some of the fleeing fruits and place them back in the bag, I take a momentary breather and rest on my hands and knees. I back up to turn, and I feel my hip bump into the woman, who is also on the ground trying to save as much of her fruit as possible.

Still on our knees with people swirling around us, we work as a team and quickly gather the rest of the fruit into her bags. The woman looks at me and begins laughing. I'm not sure what the right thing is to do, but I laugh as hard as she does. After a couple of minutes of laughing, and embarrassed, I introduce myself.

"I'm Naomi. Please forgive me for knocking your fruit over."

She says, "Naomi, it's nice to meet you. I'm Mary."

We help each other get back on our feet. "Mary, may I repay you for or replace the food you've lost?"

Mary's face has a surprised look, as if to say, "Are you kidding?"

And sure enough, that's what she says, "No, absolutely not. It was just an accident. Matter of fact, I'm glad it happened."

I am a little confused. "Why?"

"Because I feel like I met a new friend today. So, Naomi, where do you live?"

I point to the south end of the market. "Just over there, a short walk from the market. We've been here only about six months. How about you?"

"Good news, Naomi. We are practically neighbors. I live that way too. My husband, Joseph, is a carpenter. He has a small woodworking shop behind our house. Our children live with us. What about your family?"

"My husband, Aran, travels a lot, taking our goats to markets far away. He is a sort of trader, buying wares from one city and selling them in the next. We have a son, Seth. His father already has him helping in the business. I hate it when my husband takes him on sales trips for days, or weeks at a time. I don't like Seth being away from home—away from me—that long. He's still just a boy, twelve years old. I don't think he is ready to be thrust into the hard, sometimes cruel, world."

I take a step backward as a young woman pushing a cart full of apples barely misses us as she hurries by.

Mary steps toward me and resumes our conversation mother to mother. "Naomi, I know what you are saying. Our son is also twelve. It is a scary world out there. I pray for him every day. That certainly helps me not to worry as much. I think it's a mother's nature to be concerned or care about the safety and well-being of her children. I believe God will watch over him."

Aran doesn't tolerate our Jewish heritage in our home at all, so I feel awkward. Appearances, yes. We keep the Sabbath and attend the synagogue. But Aran forbids any kind of true allegiance. Our practices are only for show.

The only belief Aran has in God is what would make him get ahead in the Jewish community. Aran will go on for hours ridiculing anyone who believes they must have a god or religion in their life. I can hear it now: *All they want is your money, your time, and your allegiance to something or someone that isn't real. The only thing a person should be true to is themselves. You can never do enough to be the perfect person the religious zealots want you to be, do this, don't do that.* Aran believes you can never do enough to please the religious leaders, even if you try.

I quickly change the subject. "Mary, did you say your son helps his father in the family business?"

"No, yes . . . well, I mean . . . no, I didn't say that but yes, he does work with his father in the carpentry business."

"Mary, what's your son's name? Maybe he and Seth know each other. Seth sometimes meets kids in the neighborhood." I hear my words come out faster and faster, hoping to keep her from circling back to religion.

My distaste for certain traditions goes beyond Aran's. Tradition put Aran and me together. It wasn't a true love story, a match made in heaven. No, it was an arrangement of convenience and property. I became Aran's property in exchange for some of my grandfather's property.

"My son's name is Jesus. Yes, maybe our sons have met. Jesus certainly likes to make new friends." Mary turns slightly toward me as we continue walking out of the market. "The name of Jesus was given to us before he was even born. I know all mothers think their children are special, but Jesus is truly special. He was given to Joseph and me to introduce him to and share him with the world. I cherish every day I have with him because I know that someday, I will have to let him go and complete what he was sent here to do. So yes, I pray for him daily. Maybe I can tell you the whole story about his name someday."

We stop at Mary's street. I apologize again, and we chuckle. "Mary, I enjoyed running into you today. Seriously, I hope we can chat again sometime."

"Me too, Naomi. Now that we know where each other lives, we can get together and have some herbal tea and cake some afternoon."

"Sure, that would be great," I say, hoping she doesn't hear the reluctance in my voice. "I would love to have tea with you soon." The last thing I want is to have her over and meet Aran. She would present a discussion of God that certainly couldn't be avoided. That would be terrible. Even if I go to her house first, I will be honor-bound to return the invitation. Sadness wells inside me. I would like very much to have a friend I could talk to now and then.

Mary turns and heads down the street. But I freeze in one spot. My legs won't move. I stand there thinking about our conversation. The way she talked about her son, Jesus, differed from the way other mothers talk about their children. Her tone was filled with genuine motherly love but also with a reverent love. Maybe I should pray for Seth. Real prayers, not the fake ones that people think I'm saying when attending synagogue. I'm not sure I can believe in prayer. God didn't hear my prayers when I asked for a way out of my prearranged marriage to Aran.

Maybe I wasn't doing something right when I prayed years ago. Perhaps Mary can teach me how to pray.

My legs are still stone cold and stiff. I tilt my head toward the sky as if someone else is gently cupping my head in their hands and directing me to the heavens. The next thing I know, I am speaking out loud, "God, I don't know who you are or if you exist. I don't know how to even talk to you, but here it goes. I ask that you watch over my son, Seth. Protect him from the evils of the world and the wrath of his father. I love Seth very much, and I know he is a good person. I hope you are real and hear my prayer."

Immediately, I feel a warm sensation go through my body, and the stone-cold weight of my legs fades away. I turn toward my street and move forward, not sure what just happened, but it differs from anything I have ever experienced in my life. I feel as if someone truly heard me.

Chapter Four

Seth

It feels so good to be out today. The warmth of the sun beating down on my body helps make my back ache less. This beating is welcomed. I feel my body healing each day.

As I approach the pond, I see it—the tree. It drapes out over the water, providing the best afternoon shade and breeze a boy could want. It reminds me of the spot Father and I shared that rare special moment. We have done nothing fun together since that day.

Even though it makes me sad to think we probably will never have a moment like that again, I still like being reminded of it.

The heat of the day makes me want to jump in the pond and cool off. That will feel great. I stand up and turn toward the water's edge, kicking off my sandals. The cool water fills between my toes. I untie my belt and let my tunic slide gently down my back. Making my movements as slow as possible lessens the pain.

I hear a rustling noise off to my left. Out of the corner of my eye, I see a squirrel jumping from the branch to the tall grass resting against the tree. When I turn my head to make sure that is all it is, I catch a reflection in the water of the black and blue ridges of the scars running down my back in all directions, some as long as my arm, some the length of my fingers. The whip that was made to cause damage worked wonderfully. I stand mesmerized, looking at the reflection in the water. I want the image to be gone. The moment I step into the water, the waves part from me and that horrible description of my back is erased. If only it is that simple in real life. I wish the black and blue scars could be gone as fast as the water ripples away.

Into the deepest part of the pond, I walk and tilt so I can float. Watching the clouds go by for a long time, I scratch my nose and see my hand is all wrinkly. It's time to get out of the pond, dry off, and head back home to do chores. Standing, I step carefully through the slippery mud and land on dry ground once again. Just as I lift my soaked tunic over my shoulders, a voice from near the tree calls in my direction. "Seth, hi. How was the water? I bet it feels good on a day like today."

I was hoping to have the river all to myself today. I especially didn't want anyone to see my back. How am I going to explain the scars? Tying my tunic quickly, wincing through a sharp pain or two, I respond, "The water feels great. Jesus, what are you doing way out here?"

"None of the other kids wanted to do anything. They complained it was too hot, so I took a walk to the pond, to skip rocks, or, maybe like you, take a swim."

Hoping Jesus didn't see my back, I say, "Sorry I can't stick around. I am late. My dad was expecting me home a long time ago." I kick my feet back into my sandals and quickly head up to the walking path toward home.

But Jesus meets me on the path. Caught in an awkward situation, I stop as we make eye contact.

"Seth, if you ever need someone to talk to about anything, I want you to know you can talk to me. What you say to me stays with me."

What did Jesus mean by this? What does he know about me and my family? Jesus and I have played together with the other kids in the fields along the north end of town, but I never thought we were close friends. I don't want to have close friends. I didn't want anyone to know about my father and the life he was planning for me.

Looking down at the ground, trying to search for what to say next, or what not to say, I finally find the words. "Jesus, there is nothing you can do to help. If I live the life my father wants or demands me to live, all will be fine. If you want to help, help by leaving me alone. You have nothing to offer me that will ever be able to save me."

There I said it. That should put Jesus in his place. I'm sure he will back off now.

I turn to head down the path, when Jesus says, "Seth, you can live with the scars on your back. Over time they will heal by themselves, but the scars of a broken heart will never heal if you don't seek forgiveness. Forgiveness for your father and forgiveness from the Father."

Walking away from Jesus, warm tears slide down my cheeks. It takes everything I have not to wipe them from my face. I don't want Jesus to know the impact his words have on me. How can a boy the same age as me say things that make you think with both your mind and your heart? How is that even possible?

I think about it the entire trip home. When I approach my house, I get thrown back into reality. I hear Father shouting at Mother, and Mother crying once again. It's probably something about me, and Mother is crying for me. I will soon find out as I slowly open the back door. The creak it makes silences the room immediately. Sticking my head in first, I say, "Mother, Father, I'm home."

"It's about time!" yells my father. "Where have you been?" His face was as red as the bowl of apples sitting on the kitchen table.

Yes, I was right. Mother had gone to the market today. "Father, I was at the pond, thinking about our secret place on the Jordan." I hope Father will reminisce about our special day and quickly change from yelling to laughing. I hope he will come running over to me for a big hug. That doesn't happen.

Instead, Father grabs one of the wooden kitchen stools, yanks it out from under the table, and says, "Come over here now and sit down."

Chapter Five

Seth

"We need to talk," Father says from the kitchen table.

The large bowl of red apples sits piled high on the table next to Father. A slight breeze slips through the kitchen window, moving the curtains from side to side and cooling me off from my hurried walk home from the river.

A dutiful son, I walk over to my favorite stool. Glancing at my mother, I find some relief that I'm not alone with Father. I sit on the stool that takes me on fantasy voyages when things get tough. On board my wobbly stool I can travel to faraway places where the nicest people live, where the best food is served. I visit places in my mind where the animals don't attack; they talk to you and become your friends. Even so, I can't escape the madness at home.

This time my stool doesn't move. It doesn't rock from back to front. No bobbing in the pretend waves of the ocean that carry me from island to island. This ship is dead in the water.

I grab both sides of the stool to draw myself closer to the table and look down. I see someone has evened the legs, mooring my make-believe ship and anchoring it to a dry dock, never to sail again. Sadly, it seems my travels are over. It's back to the real world for me, where the waves of dysfunction and dread are real.

Father doesn't seem to notice or care that I am down. Why would he? He has never asked how I felt about anything going on in my life. He jumps right in with, "Seth, it's time. You are twelve now, and most boys your age go to work full-time. I was twelve when my father made me work with him in his trading business. It's time for you to do the same."

I nod numbly.

He continues. "In the spring, we'll go to Jerusalem during the Feast of the Passover. Thousands of Jews will take the yearly pilgrimage."

Father rubs his hands together. "It's ironic that the feast is a celebration of the end of slavery in Egypt and the beginning of freedom. I will free the Jewish people once again . . . this time from their possessions."

As Father speaks with glee about his upcoming conquests, Mother shakes her head in disgust. Mother does not agree with Father's means to make money. She talks to him all the time about doing something different, like moving back to somewhere with more water, enlarging the herd of goats, and perhaps buying cattle.

Many nights, after I've gone to bed, I hear them arguing about Father's plan to turn me into a younger version of himself, training me in his ways. "Seth, this is who I am, I steal, cheat, and swindle people out of their money and possessions any way I can. Now, you can be like me, or you can be whatever you want to be. It's up to you."

If I'm honest with myself, I do like working with Father sometimes. I like the thought of having a lot of money and nice things like we have now: a nice house, and nice clothes. But even more than we have would be nice. I admit I don't always like the thought of taking from people, but yes, I can get used to the nice life it can bring me when I get older.

It's like the tug of two ends of a rope. On one end, the tug into the shady life is strong, a life of lawlessness, and then the tug on the other end becomes strong, pulling me into a life of lawfulness. Which end of the rope will I end up on?

The struggle confuses me more than I wish it did. In Jericho, I didn't see my friends fighting multiple voices in their heads, being pulled into different life choices.

Matter of fact, it's just the opposite. When I think of Jesus, he seems to know exactly which end of the rope he is holding . . . but he probably doesn't have a father with a heavy hand, forcing the end of the rope he wants Jesus to hold on to. Or, Ruth, who would be just as happy being a normal, healthy girl.

"Seth!" Father shouts, "Are you listening to me?" I realize I'm looking past Father, contemplating the questions that will ultimately define who I am, who I will become, and the crosses to bear in the future. His rough tone jolts me back into the moment. My head flinches back, and I feel my eyes widen to signal, *Yes, I hear every word you are saying*. I quickly respond with the answer he wants to hear.

"Yes, I am listening. I can't wait for spring, for our trip to Jerusalem. We are going to make a killing! Father, maybe we will make enough to escape this dead-end town. This small village you said you didn't want to live in, but Mother's grandfather gave you the land, so you had to.

With a look of shock in Father's eyes, lips awkwardly curving upward in a rare attempt at a smile, he says with a hint of pride, "Yes, finally we can move back to a better town, a bigger home, and a lifestyle we deserve."

I hope so much Father will walk over to me and we will share another special moment, like that day we spent at the river. But he leans forward, grabs an apple out of the bowl, tosses it to me, and says, "Here, have an apple. You deserve it. This comforts me when I see you get excited about our future. Now, get to bed early. Tomorrow we ramp up our training for the big city."

Father gives a half-hearted smirk that says, "I told you so." He turns toward Mother and says, "See, Naomi, Seth wants to work with his father. It's a good thing. You'll be glad he does. It's only the beginning of a whole new life for all of us. Now, I'm going to have a glass or two of wine over at my buddy's house. Don't wait up for me."

Father pushes her out of his way as he passes through the kitchen, through the tiny sitting room, and heads for the front door.

Mother looks at me. Tears are streaming down her face. "Seth, no matter what you do with your life, I will always love you. And now, more than ever, I will pray for you. I will pray to God asking, no *begging*, to keep you in his hands to protect you from the dangerous and destructive evil flames of life that can consume you in a matter of moments."

Before I can say anything, she backs out the door leading from the kitchen to the small alley in the back of our house and is gone.

I am now by myself in the kitchen. "Praying for me?" I say out loud while staring out the square window where the air is as still as I am. There is not even a slight movement of the curtains that once danced in all directions. The sun drops lower and lower outside, and the room fills with darkness.

I reach for a candle on the table and walk over to the kitchen fire pit to light it. Returning to my stool, the glow stretches up off the top of the wax-dripped candle. As I lean back on my stool, I realize I am still holding the apple Father tossed me. Looking closer at it, I notice flames dancing around the shiny red covering. Immediately, I jerk the apple away from the flame, wanting to protect it, to keep it away from the dangers dancing over its skin, soon realizing it had not caught on fire. It was the flame bouncing from the top of the candle reflecting its hot fiery glow, looking as if it was attacking the apple without mercy. It was safe in my hands the whole time.

Wow! This is crazy. Mother just said she would pray for me. For me to be kept safe in God's hands from the destruction of the evils of the fiery flames of life. This is too close for comfort. I jump up and blow the candle out. As soon as the flame goes out, the curtains hanging at the top of the window blow wide open, from the inside of the kitchen, flapping outside of the window, letting a glimmer of light from the moon drop to the kitchen floor. *Strange*, I think, *there is no breeze to be felt coming in or going out.* I drop the apple back in the bowl and run, jumping in my bed. Throwing the covers over my head I hope Mother will come back home soon . . . very soon.

Chapter Six

Aran

My mind runs in circles like wild dogs trying to catch their tails. That could be because of the strong drink I just had with my *"never enough"* drinking buddies. But I know part of it is the back-and-forth I had with Naomi. When it comes to Seth, I am trying to be a good father and make him into a man like my father wanted me to be. She fights me every step of the way. All she wants to do is coddle him like a baby. This tough world will chew him up and spit him out if he doesn't learn to fight for what he wants. I think he wants what I am trying to prepare him for. As my father would say to me, "Life is hard, and then you die." I want Seth to get more out of life than just to survive.

Forget the wine and being around my friends, loud raucous men with too much strong drink in their bellies already. I need to leave this house and go somewhere to clear my head.

I head down a path lit up by moonlight popping through the clouds. The night is beautiful. A cool breeze brushes across the tall grass lining both sides of the narrow path. I see a lone tree with a nice canopy of branches hanging out away from its trunk, making for a nice getaway place to sit down, catch my breath, and just stop running in my mind. As I lean up against the tree, letting the cool evening breeze drift across my body, my mind drifts off to the time I took

Seth fishing. It was a beautiful river outside the village we lived in before moving to Nazareth.

By far, this was my favorite place when I needed to get away from everything and everybody. My go-to place when I needed to escape the reality of a cruel world crashing down on me.

I took Seth there to fish a time or two. Thinking of that river brings back a lot of memories, both good and bad. I used to sit on the riverbank under the huge tree hanging out over the river. A big smooth stone weathered perfectly over the years makes for a great place to sit and watch the river go by. I would sit down to relax, letting the stresses of the day escape.

The stone by the river had cradled my body as if it were specially made for me. I remember the first time I sat in it. My father brought me there to fish, and he told me a story of how the stone got there. He told me it was a royal throne, made for him by the people of the land for being the best fisherman alive. Catching the largest and most fish, enough to feed all the people in town and the surrounding towns. As an eight-year-old, I had no reason not to believe what he was telling me.

Father was a tall man, built like a warrior. His arms were filled with muscles, his shoulders stretched wide, as wide as the banks of that river. His legs looked like he could carry the heaviest of loads. I didn't get any of his physical traits. Many people would tease me and say mean things about being the runt of the family. I wanted, wished, and even prayed to God at the synagogue he would make me like my father.

Nothing changed, and that's when I gave up on God. I remember trying to build muscles by picking up heavy sacks of grain and carrying them on my back, hoping to get big and strong like Father. Nothing worked. Father would laugh, joining all the other people to make fun of me. I wanted so much for Father to be proud of me.

The greatest fisherman in the world. That's what Father wanted me to believe. I eventually learned that it wasn't true. Father wasn't a giver he was a taker. His goal in life was to take whatever he could from whomever he could. I also discovered early in life that if I didn't do what Father wanted me to do or do it good enough, I would get the right adjustment necessary. I know full well how the two-and-half-foot scourge feels ripping my back from top to bottom.

I don't know why I do the same things to Seth as my father did to me. The rage that fills me is not rage for Seth; it's the rage I feel toward my father. Why couldn't my father and mother teach me how to love someone just as easily as they showed me how to hate?

Mother wasn't like Naomi either, a loving, caring mother. No, she would laugh at me just as much as everyone else. All I wanted was my parents' approval, acceptance . . . love. I got none. I don't hate Seth or Naomi, I just don't know how to love them.

Tears are coming faster and faster now. My tunic feels as if I have fallen into a river.

Now I can't stop laughing because of the wet tunic. I remember the time Seth and I were fishing at the Jordan River. I fought gallantly for the one prized fish of the day, moving side to side, trying to find the right spot to land the warrior of all fighting fish. My feet got crossed up, and I hit the water head-first. Popping up for air, I held the trophy high over my head, shouting, "I got it! I got it!"

I called Seth over to help me get out of the waist-deep water since I had my hands filled with a fishing pole in one hand and the conquest in the other. This little scraggly boy came running over to help rescue me. When he reached me, he leaned as far as he could. We grabbed hands. I took one step forward when the mud under my other foot caused me to slip backward, and in the water we both went. Down went Seth, his arms pounding the water, doing all he could to resurface. I reached down to pick him up and held him securely against my chest. Realizing how frightened Seth was, I wanted him to feel safe and taken care of.

Gulping for air and spitting out water in my face, he opened his eyes and looked right into mine. With an expression of fear that he was going to drown, his face immediately changed to a smile and relief. We both laughed until we cried.

A part of me is a little sad that I never had an experience like that with my father. As I think back to that day at the river with Seth, I am a little sad I never had another moment like that one with him.

Since tears are running down my cheeks, I am glad it's dark under the tree and no one is around.

Enough of all this father-son special moment stuff. It's time to get back home. Back to the real world of training up a son to fend for himself, to go get what is due to him. The weak will die. That is why I must treat him the way I do, I must make him strong, stronger than I have ever been. If Seth is looking for a loving father, he will have to look somewhere else. But not to religion. The one, and only, time I went to those who called themselves religious for help, to escape the daily verbal and physical beatings from my parents, they turned their backs on me. They didn't care for me, or show love or mercy. No, not one who professed to love God showed any love to me. No one was interested in saving a little boy in need of a savior.

From that day on, I said, if that is how the God-loving people treat people like me I will never have anything to do with their God. No, I will do whatever I must to keep Seth from believing the religious people in the synagogues. They turned their backs on me. I blame them for letting me go down the path that left me out and hanging with nowhere to go. Maybe my life wouldn't be what it is today, and I could be the loving father Naomi wants me to be if just one Jewish leader had reached out to me. I must protect Seth from any false hope that a follower of God cares about him . . . can save him. The only person who can save you is yourself.

It's getting late. I have to get home. An early morning is waiting for me. Stepping away from the tree, I feel the soreness of leaning against it for too long. I shake my right foot awake and grab the low-hanging branch—the one right in front of me. It's as if it is reaching out to give me that hand I needed when I was that helpless boy.

Chapter Seven

Seth

Spears of bright light cut through the small holes in my wool blanket, jabbing me right in my eyes. Jolted out of a deep sleep, I feel relief knowing I survived the night with scary thoughts swirling in my mind. I had tossed and turned most of the night, thinking about the fiery red apple and mother saying she would pray for me. Mother prays that God would keep me safe from evil. Plus, seeing the curtains in the kitchen window flapping around when there wasn't a breeze to be felt, had me thinking all sorts of scary things. Was there something evil trying to get me?

I pull my blanket off one eye and look around my room to confirm the light is nothing more than the sun peeking through my bedroom window. Yes! I'm alive!

The aroma of barley cakes cooking in the kitchen brings me comfort. I can smell the sweet scent of honey and imagine a mound of butter running down the side of a tall stack of cakes. I can close my eyes, and no matter where I am, this smell always brings me back home to the kitchen with Mother. I know then I am loved and safe, at least for a moment.

I peel the blanket off my other eye, yanking the rest of the arrows of light away from me, and jump up out of bed. I slap my feet into my sandals and trot toward the smell of my favorite breakfast calling my name.

"Good morning, Mother. Wow! Those cakes sure smell great."

Mother is startled by my booming voice as I approach the kitchen. She jumps backward, doing everything she can to keep from losing her balance and hitting the floor while holding a beautiful tower of barley cakes swaying side to side. Her hands quickly move to catch up with them. She has a look of determination not to lose one cake, even if it means she must sacrifice herself to save the tower.

With all cakes secure in their rightful place, Mother looks at me. She is dazed, but still standing upright.

"Seth! Why do you do that to me? You're going to make my heart pop right out of my body if you don't stop sneaking up on me like that."

With guilt and not wanting an accident to befall my cakes, I reach and grab the plate from Mother's hands and gently rest the plate on the table. With a sigh of relief, more so for the potential fate of my cakes, I say, "Mother, I am so sorry I startled you. I didn't mean to scare you like that."

As if on cue, we burst out laughing. It feels good to laugh and have someone to laugh with.

Mother chuckles and gestures to the chair. "Sit down and eat your pancakes before they get cold."

She didn't have to tell me twice. With a tall mug of milk on one side and a heap of butter on the other side of my tower of cakes, I dig in. The room becomes quiet again. Mother is back to working in the kitchen. I recall the cake-plate mishap and feel a smile coming on my face. I love to laugh.

Mother and I laugh together a lot. Mainly because I think she wants me to have happiness, and to share some fun times. She wants me to be a normal kid. Mother can always make me laugh, especially when she tells me stories about her childhood.

She grew up in a typical labor-class family. They didn't have a lot, but they made do with what they had. Her father worked as a farmhand and her mother wove and sold clothes at their local market.

Mother did some crazy stuff as a kid. Not bad stuff, just risky things her brothers would dare her to do. She told me once they dared her to ride a donkey that they knew wasn't broke for riding. With help from her brothers, she got up on it, and they let go. The donkey took off bucking while twisting back and forth. She held on for dear life. Her brothers couldn't believe she was still sitting on the back of this donkey and not lying face down in the dirt. Of course, she and her father had already been working with this donkey so she knew what was coming. She teased them for days about how good she was at riding and how they were too afraid to get on it.

My favorite story, however, is the one about her pet hyrax, also known as rabbits or hares. Mother told me they had a pet hyrax that loved her but was not a fan of her brothers. They would tease it, and play rough with it. One time when her brothers were asleep, her father kept calling for them to get up and do the chores. Mother went out and got the hyrax. It was pretty big for most hyraxes. It had sharp teeth, and its claws could cause a scratch or two if it got agitated. She put it under their blanket in the bed they all slept in together. The hyrax was doing everything it could to get out from under the blanket, scratching and clawing its way out. Her brothers couldn't get out of bed fast enough. They shouted and leaped, gyrating, flailing their arms and legs around as if they were being attacked by a hundred wild animals.

Mother laughed so hard while telling me that story she cried, waving her hands in the air as if mimicking what she had seen her brothers doing that morning. She always punctuated her story by adding, "And they thought Father did it!"

With only one cake left, Mother walks over and sits down with a cup of hot water flavored with figs. She looks at my plate in disbelief, "You ate all of them? Didn't save any for me?"

Feeling a little ashamed, I lift the plate with the one lonely pancake left and offer it to her.

Cracking a smile, she responds, "Just kidding. I had my tower before you were out of bed."

We both laugh.

"Seth, I know you are going to be working with your father more." Mother holds the cup close to her lips and blows the steam off the top. "I just want you to know you don't have to be like him." She takes a sip from the cup. "I could send you to one of my brothers, and you can live with him and his family. Your father couldn't care less where any of them live and besides, they are not afraid of him. If they knew how he treats us, they would be here so fast your head would spin."

I am in shock and left speechless. Why is she telling me this?

"I know your father would be very upset at me if that happened. His wrath would come down on my back as it has on yours. My utmost desire is to keep you safe. To give you a better life, a life away from stealing and cheating others. But I don't know if I can do it." She takes another sip.

Pushing the plate away with the solitary cake, I see a shadow pass by the kitchen window. The door opens, and Father walks in with an angry look on his face. Without acknowledging Mother, he stares right at me and barks out orders. "Seth, let's go. You have wasted too much of the day already."

As I push the chair back from the table, I see Mother take another sip of her drink. Speaking over the edge of the cup with both hands wrapped and overlapping. Holding the cup close to her face, she concludes with, "Seth, please don't say anything to your father about what I just said."

I wonder how long Father had been lingering by the window. Had he heard Mother talking about my going to live with one of her brothers?

"Seth! Come on!" Father says louder.

Playing what Mother just told me around in my head. I go from should I leave? Should I stay with Father? If I go live with Mother's brothers, I know my life will be safe but probably not exciting. They are simple farmers with simple lives. Father's paths offer adventure, excitement, and most of all, riches. I know what I'm going to do. Right or wrong I'm going with Father. I can only hope it will be the right decision. Who knows? Maybe Father and I someday will have the real father-son relationship that I long for. I want that even more than any riches.

Chapter Eight

Seth
The month of Nisan

I love springtime! The month of Nisan is here. Flowers hiding from the chilly nights have blossomed, taking in the warm breeze and sun of the day. It is my favorite time of the year. It reminds me of a new start, new beginnings for the things of this world. It's as if the world offers do-overs. The things that die in one season erupt to life in another. A fresh start. A new life. It's okay to come back out to live, play, and be seen once again.

It's time for Father and me to head to Jerusalem. We have been planning diligently these past six months, meeting with others who will help us pull off what might be our biggest heist so far. Plus, Father and I have been on the road for many weeks traveling from village to village. Up to now, we have only been conning small amounts of money from trusting people who think they are going to make lots of money investing in our made-up trading opportunities.

Within days, the streets of Jerusalem will swell from a daily population of thirty to fifty thousand to well over two million. All those additional people will be on their pilgrimage to the temple, participating in their annual Feast of Passover or the Pesach celebration. They also come prepared to pay their annual tax for the upkeep of the temple.

An abundance of money will be passing through hands during the eight days of the celebration. The main participants in all these transactions are Money Changers, as Father calls them. Their main purpose is to convert the Roman currency into Tyrian shekels. The Roman coins are only 80 percent silver, while the Tyrian shekels are 94 percent or higher. The Tyrian shekel was required to pay the temple tax in Jerusalem.

With the tremendous amount of people in Jerusalem comes a colossal amount of money. And that is why Father and I are here. We plan to help ourselves to as much of the temple tax money as possible. The bounty should be more than anything we have stolen in the past.

As we approach the main gate of Jerusalem, Father stands on the opposite side of the road with his right arm, motioning me to move ahead of a large caravan of people approaching the gate. The travelers seem to be near the end of their long journey. If we don't beat them to the gate, we will be stuck outside looking at one pack after another pack of Jewish people parading up to the city's main gate. It would take us hours to follow them in.

It is kind of funny watching Father "run" with his short, chunky legs, arms pumping back and forth. The motion makes him look like an ostrich trying to take flight but does nothing to help him move faster. Every three or four steps he reaches up and grabs the striped fabric wrapped around the top of his head as it droops to one or the other side of his head with each awkward step. It takes everything I have to not burst out laughing at him.

We make it through the gate by the skin of our teeth, and a man, with his robe tightly around his head and face, is standing off to the side, waving us over to follow him down a path. It is covered by thick trees and high grass, and I reason that few know of its existence. One step in, and we are out of sight.

As we hurry around the branches and through the tall grass, the mystery man and Father push back on the tree limbs to clear a path, only to let the branches go, so I get smacked in the face relentlessly. I imagine the trees are laughing at me, mocking and spitting as the morning dew flings from the pine tree needles into my mouth and eyes.

Without any warning, the bright sun bursts into my eyes as the last branch swoops past me. I am so glad to be out of the jungle. The stranger points to a covered wooden cart pulled by one over-sized ox. Without missing a beat, Father jumps in the back, turns, and stretches his arm out to me. He grabs hold of me, and in an instant, I am lying face down next to him. As the cart moves, I look at Father and he presses his stubby finger against his lips, his eyes open wide. Without saying a word, he lets me know to be silent.

We slowly pass through the city and with every bounce of the cart, I'm reminded we are not on a pleasure trip. No, I am going to be sore after we get to wherever we are going if the ride in the cart doesn't beat me to death first.

I can hear voices all around as we pass by. A man selling his wares by the street. A woman's voice yelling at a young child to be careful, to watch where they are going. Men laughing as if someone told the funniest story ever. Chatter coming at me from all directions.

The noise level is higher than I have ever experienced. Still lying on my stomach, I turn my head to the right and peek through a rip in the worn wool covering that smells as if it has doubled as the long-time blanket of the old, oversized ox. I didn't know what to cover, my nose or ears. It's crazy how crowded the streets are.

The cart stops. The stranger peeks through the back of the covering and motions for us to follow him. Father wiggles his way out; I follow Father. We quickly walk to a stone structure that is larger than any other nearby building. Our tour guide—the stranger who has yet to introduce himself—goes up ahead of us and says something to the guards standing in front of a massive metal door. After a short conversation, he motions for us to come to him. He hands a torch to my father. Father and I follow closely behind our guide.

It is so dark that without the bright torches, I doubt I could see anything in front of me. I peek in before the torch is handed to Father. It is the darkest place I have ever been in. I have been in caves that were not as dark as this place. Being a little afraid, I wait for Father to go in ahead of me, grabbing his robe to stay close. We head down a narrow stone path. It curves to the left and slopes downward. I see massive walls squeezing us in as the torch flames bounce off the stones. The saving grace of this whole scary experience is the dampness, which cools off the tunnel providing relief from the heat of the day.

No sooner does that thought cross my mind when the mystery man stops without warning, causing Father to abruptly halt on a Tyrian shekel. And I, of course, am daydreaming, so I bang right into Father's back, which causes him to dance around to avoid dropping his torch. Even in the shadows of the semidarkness, I can see his frustrated expression.

"Boy, watch where you are going," he says while pushing me back a step or two.

With torch securely in Father's hand, we step into a large room where candles line the walls from top to bottom. Once my eyes adjust to the light, I stand motionless and see trunk after trunk pressed against the walls. Father runs over to one and lifts the lid. We can see the precious metals of gold and silver shekels nearly overflowing. Now it hits me. This is not just where they keep the temple tax money, but this must be the treasury chamber where King Herod stores all his money, too. And I'm standing inside it. I don't know if I should cry, laugh, or pass out. This is it. Is this going to be our big payoff?

Father turns to me, grabs me by both arms, and picks me up. "Seth, someday we are coming back to get all of this." Father spins me around so I can see the vast amount of money lining the walls.

Father continues. "The man who brought us here is an old friend of mine. He is commissioned as a guard to watch over this place. He told me if we do a good job at the temple treasury chamber, this can be our next robbery—the robbery of a lifetime!"

Being at eye level with Father, I see tears fill his eyes. "Seth, this is what I want for you, me, your mother. This is it. We will be able to have whatever we want! We won't have to ever work again. No more little schemes here and there. No more traveling for weeks at a time going from one filthy village to another. No more herding goats. We deserve this new life of fortune."

He sets me back down on solid ground. I smile at him, not saying a word. But wondering to myself, will it be enough for him? Will this provide me and Father the happiness we are looking for? If I help him with this robbery, will that make me enough in his eyes? And do we really deserve it? Or do we just desire it?

Chapter Nine

Mary

"Jesus, where are you?"

I pop my head around the kitchen wall, looking for him. "Come on," I shout. "It's getting late. We should have been on the road an hour ago."

I don't hear any response like, "Okay Mother, I'll be right there." No, nothing.

The door opens quickly, startling me. Joseph looks at me as if I am out of my mind and says, "Mary, your son, has been patiently waiting for over two hours by the cart. Jesus is more eager to leave than you are."

I look at Joseph, surprised. "That's odd. Why is he in such a hurry to get to Jerusalem?"

Joseph turns and shrugs his shoulders. "I don't know, but we'd better go now before he takes off without us."

As we arrive in Jerusalem, I see how packed the city is. From attending past festivals, I know the city is filled with worshipers, wanderers, and the wicked. All are coming together, but not all with the same motives, the same reasons. Some are here to give. Some are here to get. I certainly hope Jesus will be okay in the middle of all this madness. Vendors selling their wares pack the streets. Mixed in the crowds of people walking are children running and playing with friends they haven't seen in a year. On many of the street corners, there are men with their hands reaching to the sky, preaching the scrolls of the temple to whoever might listen. Most are passed unnoticed.

It is a time when you can either get lost in the madness, be part of the madness, ignore the madness, or challenge the madness. Joseph and I hope we can provide Jesus with a sense of calmness in all the festival madness.

When you combine the many voices; the clunking noise of the wooden cartwheels going up and down the street; music playing at certain drinking establishments; and the shouting of the temple scribes on the street corners, it begins to sound like the high-pitched noise of a sandstorm booming across the desert.

The city noise is never-ending. The only place to find some calmness is the temple courtyard. Jesus made it clear the entire journey here that he wanted to spend a lot of time at the temple. Every day during the Feast of the Passover, teachers and scholars sit around the courtyard and talk about religious teachings, writings, and laws given by God. The God we proclaim created the heavens and the earth, man and woman, and all that is in it. It's the same God who delivered our people from the bonds of slavery.

At times, the conversation can become lively, bordering on argumentative. On the way here, Jesus told us how much he was looking forward to hearing the discussions and that he might have a thing or two to say as well. What on earth does a twelve-year-old boy have to say?

Day after day, Jesus was up and out of the house early. Joseph and I wondered why he was so eager to get to the temple each day. We asked him, and he would say as he excitedly backed out the door, "I have so many questions!"

———— • ● • ————

The Feast of the Passover ended yesterday after eight full days of celebration. I love coming to Jerusalem and spending time with my aunt and uncle. They are great hosts and treat us like royalty, but it's time to head back home. I am tired. I hope the children we had to leave in Nazareth are okay.

The cart is loaded. Goodbyes and hugs seem to go on forever. It's bittersweet to leave so many friends and family members we see only once a year.

On the dusty road about eight hours out of the city, half asleep from the hypnotic rhythm of the cart's wheels, I realize something: I do not see Jesus. Fully awake, I rise and ask Joseph, "Have you seen Jesus?"

"No, I thought you knew where he was."

"No, I don't. The last time I saw him, he was talking to his friend Seth, and I assumed Jesus was going to travel with Seth and his father back home."

"Jesus told me Seth and his father were staying in the city a few more days to set up some trading partnerships. I thought Jesus found another friend to travel with, and he told you."

Now I'm feeling agitated. "No, Joseph, your son did not tell me he was traveling with a friend. Joseph, I think you went off and left your son behind"

"Me! I think *you* left your son behind. I thought you knew what was going on."

I look at Joseph and shake my head, knowing I am more right than he is. "Well, it doesn't matter who is right or wrong. We have to turn around right now and head back to Jerusalem and find the son you forgot."

Without saying another word, Joseph tugs on the donkey's reins, and back we go. Not another word is uttered on the long and painfully silent journey back to Jerusalem.

Now back where we started and feeling embarrassed, I knock on the door of Aunt Esther and Uncle Abe's house. Very gingerly, the door opens.

Aunt Esther peeks her head around the door. "Mary, it's so good to see you again. What happened? Did you forget something? I found one of your capes lying in the corner of the room. Wait here. I'll go get it for you."

With a fake smile and a chuckle, I say, "No, no, Aunt Esther. Well, it's kind of hard to admit, but we think we left without Jesus. We were hoping he was still here, with you and Uncle Abe.

Aunt Esther can't hold back any longer. She bursts out laughing. "Yes, you sure left him! The word going around town is Jesus is the talk of the temple."

"The talk of the temple? What do you mean?" I ask.

Aunt Esther turns and limps to her favorite chair in the corner. With age come aches and pains in both her knees. She motions for me to join her.

"Well, there have been all kinds of discussions about scriptures, religious laws, you name it, they are talking about it. But this is what the talk is about. Your son, Jesus, is wowing them with his strong and wise understanding of everything they discuss and debate. The high priest, teachers, and scholars on the subject are amazed at Jesus' knowledge and understanding of the scriptures and teachings of the law. He even has the political sect weighing in on some of the religious discussions. Some have said they are concerned about Jesus' safety if he keeps talking like he is. Many have said no twelve-year-old boy should know and speak the way Jesus does. That's why your Uncle Abe isn't here now. He is in the temple courtyard, looking out for him, so nothing bad happens to him."

A jolt of fear runs through my body. I turn to my husband."We must hurry and get Jesus out of the temple."

Joseph grabs my hand, and with a tone of a truce in his voice says, "Yes, let's go. Let's get our son and head home now."

Joseph and I run to the temple as fast as we can, hoping we will rescue him before anything bad happens if it hasn't already.

With the celebration over and most people heading back to their homes, there are still so many gathered at the temple courtyard that we cannot get through. Joseph and I get close enough to see Jesus sitting there surrounded by the high priest and teachers.

Everyone is intent on hearing what is being said, the stillness allows Jesus' voice to reach the farthest edge of the crowd as if he is standing right next to you.

Out of the corner of my eye, I see Jesus' friend Seth slumping behind a pillar. It looks as if he is listening with sincere interest wanting to hear what Jesus is saying, but he does not want to be noticed. Maybe Seth is not hiding from Jesus, but from his father, who hates the teachings of the Torah.

After an hour of listening to my son, I still don't understand where he learned the things he is saying. Joseph and I squirm our way past the crowd and reach Jesus. With a frustrated tone, I ask, "Son, why have you treated us this way? Your father and I have been worried sick looking for you."

Jesus looks at me and says, "Why is it you were looking for me? Did you not know that I had to be in my Father's house?"

My head bent forward, looking down at his feet with a feeling of guilt, I am sorry to say I don't have a clue what he means.

Chapter Ten

Seth

It is hours after I left the temple courtyard and Jesus' blathering. Thankfully, the night is darker than most this time of year. On some evenings, even a half-moon can light up the city and the roads leaving Jerusalem. With clouds tightly gathered together like a blanket thrown over the city, the darkness will make this the best night for us to steal the temple bounty and get out of town.

"Seth, where have you been?" Father snaps at me, not happy that I am only now showing up for our big job. "You were supposed to be here an hour ago. You'd better get it together, get your head on straight, and focus on what we've been planning for. If I need to beat it into you, I will." He pounds one fist into the other, so I know he means it.

I had been thinking about what Jesus said, and I lost all sense of time. Jesus got my attention earlier, all right. He talked about how some people want to live their lives making excuses for doing wrong things.

His words echo in my head. I can still see Jesus on his feet, lifting his arms. His words seemed to have more power and passion behind them than I have ever heard before. The priests and elders were looking at one another as if they couldn't believe this twelve-year-old boy was schooling them on their own teachings. Some looked on with excitement while others looked on with disbelief, not liking everything Jesus was telling them.

Jesus would turn side to side, making sure everyone around heard what he was saying.

He explained envy can also be like jealousy. Someone has something you want. A desire to be like others, for example, can cause envy.

Jesus said it was okay to have goals, to aspire for things in life, but it's how you live your life, trusting in God to provide for your needs. You may want a big house with many cattle on a hillside. Jesus said, "Trust God. All the cattle on hill after hill belong to him. If you are his child, that, too, is your inheritance. God desires to pour His grace to quench the sinful desires that turn you away from him."

I finally force myself to stand, even climbing up a couple of branches so I can see over the crowds of people.

The crowd is inching closer and closer to hear Jesus' words. He points at them, saying, "It has been written, an arrogant man or woman stirs up strife, but he or she who trusts in the Lord will prosper. He or she who trusts in his or her own heart is a fool, but he or she who walks wisely will be delivered."

Pausing a second, Jesus looks down at his feet, his lips moving but no one can hear him. Then he raises his head with a look of sadness. "The righteousness of the upright will deliver them, but the treacherous will be caught by their greed."

Wow! That hits close to home. Father and I are here in Jerusalem to do our biggest robbery. Yet, now I have the profound words of Jesus rolling around in my head. Maybe I should go ahead, do this one theft, and then do no more. Maybe I should take my part of the spoils and run for the hills and start a new life with Mother. Maybe I will give a small portion of my money back to the temple to make it right. You know, to cover any guilt I might have afterward.

Jesus' words aren't the only ones in my head. I also can't get rid of Father's voice: "Everybody takes from others in some way or another. This is our way to even the scales of life."

I left the courtyard hours ago, thinking, *thanks, Jesus, for causing all this confusion in my head. Should I go through with the robbery tonight? Or run for the hills? Boy, I wish I had never listened to what you were talking about. It's not just a head spinner, but I feel this tugging at my heart. I can't explain what is going on. Which one will win? My head or heart?*

But when I meet Father outside the temple gate I say, "Father, I'm sorry I'm late. Let's go. I'm ready to do it."

Head one. Heart zero.

"Okay, Seth, let's go," he answers, no longer wanting to thrash me. "I'm sure the others will be waiting for us near the treasury at the Golden Gate. We don't have a lot of extra time."

I run ahead to a prearranged spot just outside the Golden Gate. I prepare to play the role of a young boy in need to distract the two temple guards. That way my father and the other two men can get to the temple treasury and into the storeroom where this week's celebration offerings and temple tax money are being held. Tomorrow morning soldiers will move it to Herod's large, dark treasury chamber Father and I saw a few days ago. We could not take anything from there on this trip because it is too well guarded. We only got in for that rare look because a guard Father knows— the mysterious stranger—snuck us in. Father has mentioned someday that might be our next big opportunity. He says, "Patience! It will still be there when we want it."

But for the treasury at the temple, our best window of opportunity is tonight during the guard shift change. We know there will be fewer guards on duty because of the king's need for extra security at his palace during the festival. Plus, Father's guard friend found out that two of the guards had never worked the temple before. You would think there would be many guards watching over the taxes. Oh well, that's okay with us. Fewer and inexperienced is better.

Everyone is in his place. One of Father's partners is a short, muscular man in his twenties. He's fast and agile, able to carry heavy loads. The other man is older, thirties maybe, able to handle the ox with ease.

I am hiding behind a tree just outside the Golden Gate. The palms of my hands are wet with nervous sweat. Drops of it run down the side of my face, and I haven't even moved yet. Am I scared or excited? Both.

With everyone in his place ready to go, I see the two guards greeting their replacements for the night. This is my cue to move in and give them the performance of my life so Father and his accomplices can sneak past.

"Help! Please help me!" I cry as I approach the guards with dirt spread all over my face as if I have been fighting. They turn toward me, away from the sight of the three men running behind them through the Golden Gate with two small pushcarts.

"What's wrong?" one of the guards asks.

Tears stream down my face, turning the dirt on my face into mud. "Three men attacked my mother and me," I wail. "They took my mother and ran in that direction." I point down a long, winding path away from the temple and say, "Please, you must help her. She is all I have. Please help me get her back!"

The guards look at one another, and without hesitating, each one takes off running. One sprints down the path to the right, nearly running into a signpost indicating the direction of the town's market. Another one takes off down the path to the left. I see him pass the water fountain that is just off the path in the temple garden. I thought for a second the sword on his waistband was going to bounce, hit it, and knock it over.

A thin guard takes the center path, with a fourth following close behind. So close I thought they might trip over each other. I look around and realize I am all alone. Not one guard stayed behind. To my pleasant surprise, all four were off and running, searching for Mother in the dark.

I feel good luck is on our side. That was easier than I hoped it would be. I thought at least one, maybe two guards would stay back.

Yes! This is exciting. "Hurry, Father," I say out loud, hoping he will appear sooner than later. I'm not sure how far or for how long the guards will search for Mother. I go from pure excitement to sheer nervous fear.

After what seems to be a long time of waiting for Father and the others to come out of the temple treasury chamber, I hear voices coming up the path that passes in front of the temple fountain leading toward the temple. I hear men arguing. The guards are debating what happened and which path the bad guys must have taken with my imaginary mother.

At about the same time, I hear what sounds like Father and his partners rolling carts toward me. *Oh no! What can I do to send the guards down another path?*

I wave to my father, hoping he can see me motion to them to wait. My hands say, "Stop, Don't move." Thankfully, he understands and pauses, blending into the gray night. That will probably be the only time I can tell my father what to do. It feels good and odd at the same time.

I turn and run to meet the guards a little way down the path just this side of the fountain. I hope to slow them down before they make it back to the temple. "Oh," I say, fear in my voice, "It is you! A man just came by and said that just moments ago, three men took a woman, who was screaming and fighting to get away. They went in that direction." I point down the path that leads to the marketplace, hoping they still want to be heroes for Mother.

The guards look at one another. Some are angry, others are befuddled. One of them shouts, "I told you that was the path we should have taken, let's go." Like sheep, they follow one another and run down the path.

With the guards out of sight, I turn back to Father and motion as if to say, "Go . . . go . . . hurry!" Again, I tell Father what to do. *I can get used to this. Or can I?* I decide to enjoy the moment believing it may never happen again.

Father and his two partners roll the carts and head down a path leading to a nearby wheat storehouse. I head down the path behind them. Waiting for us are two donkeys tied to the back of the storehouse. Once we harnessed the two beasts, off we go.

As far as I know, the guards are still looking for Mother.

What a rush this night has been. I have felt fear, excitement, and an energy level never experienced before. I feel as if I can do anything I want now.

One feeling I don't have is . . . regret.

Chapter Eleven

Seth

We did it! We robbed the temple and made it back home without anyone knowing. Mother does not know what we've accomplished or she is in denial. Most likely she doesn't want to know.

But she is a lot smarter than Father gives her credit for. That's *his* denial. We are one big, happy family of disguises and delusions. I wonder if any of us will ever admit to what is real or if we will continue playing the game of life according to our own rules.

I understand what is real or at least what feels real to me. For the first time, Father seems to be proud of me. Since we returned home, more than once Father has patted me on the back with pride, touching the same spots that are raised with the scars he inflicted and telling me what a great job I did. His words are more powerful than any lashing I have ever endured. Have I finally done enough? Am I good enough now? Having his approval is worth more than ten times the amount of money in the biggest treasury chamber in the world. That is priceless. I never really knew how much I needed that from the man I'd wished was dead on many occasions.

Tears well in my eyes and my heart beats faster as I realize the man I sometimes loathe is the same man I sometimes love.

A knock at the front door snaps me out of my thoughts. I take both hands and wipe away the tears sliding down my cheeks, getting rid of any evidence I was crying. Twelve-year-old boys, soon to turn thirteen, don't cry.

"Yes, give me a second. I will be right there," I yell across the room. I wonder who it is. I don't want to talk to anyone right now, but it might be someone for Father.

I grab the handle and open the door. Standing on the porch is the last person I want to see. "Jesus, hi." I look past him, not meeting his eyes. "What's going on?"

I hope he doesn't notice my surprised look.

"Hi, Seth, I was walking around, seeing if anyone was out, wanting to do something. No one is out, so I thought I would come by to see how you're doing. See if you wanted to play a game or something."

"Oh, I'm fine. Father and I just returned from Jerusalem. My father works me to death, so I'm pretty wiped—I mean tired."

"Yes, Seth, I knew you were back in town. Your mother was at our house, and she said you were back home. I hope you and your father got what you wanted in Jerusalem."

"We did." Looking away from Jesus. I didn't want Jesus to sense the guilt washing through my body at this very moment. Why would Mother be visiting with Jesus' mother? I didn't even know they knew each other. This can't be good. I feel hot all over as if my body is going to burst into flames at any moment. Strangely, I have this feeling of guilt. I wish I hadn't ever heard what Jesus was saying in the temple courtyard.

"How about you?" I ask. "Was your trip to Jerusalem a good one?"

"Yes, it was great. Something funny happened, though. My family went off and left me in Jerusalem. They traveled a day and then had to turn around and come back and get me. They lost two days of travel and spent a day looking for me." Jesus smiled at the memory and laughed, though he was laughing at the irony, not that his parents had been inconvenienced.

I chuckle along with Jesus, trying to show him I am enjoying the conversation.

"Your family forgot you?" I ask.

Still, with good humor, Jesus continues the story. "I spent a lot of time in the temple courtyard listening and talking to the teachers and priests, and my parents simply went off without me. But my uncle finally found me, and my aunt told them where I was."

Jesus suddenly turns solemn. "You know, Seth, I thought I saw you one day in the courtyard, sitting behind a pillar."

"No, that couldn't have been me," I reply. The lie slides out so effortlessly I even surprise myself. It is as easy as drinking a cup of cool water. "I was too busy working with my father. I never had the time to do something like that."

"Oh, that's interesting," Jesus says, looking me directly in the eyes. "Your father had time. He was there for several days. Once, he shared a thought or two about the conversation. He's not a big believer in the goodness of God. Matter of fact, he has strong beliefs that if there's a God, he should be doing more for his people."

I feel I have to defend my father. "He resents paying the temple tax. He says God shouldn't need our money. He says the priests want to make you live a life full of rules no one can possibly follow. Do this, don't do that. It doesn't matter, you can never do enough, to be good enough. A person's life is in their own hands, and they should go ahead and live the life that they want to live. God should want his people to be happy."

"Seth, is that what you believe?"

"Mostly. I guess. Sometimes I don't know what I believe or what I should believe. I try to be a good person by doing what my father tells me to do. But then you come around talking about loving God, and it confuses me again. I would prefer if you would stop talking about it. Just drop it. I don't want to talk about it anymore." My voice raises to a level that surprises even me. I am getting angry, not at Jesus so much, but at the fight going back and forth in my mind. What's right? What's wrong? It's not just my mind, I feel it in my heart sometimes.

"Seth, sorry about making you upset. I care about you and your family, and I want what's best for all of you. God doesn't want to guilt anyone into following Him. What God has to offer the world is not a religion for people to sign up for, but a real relationship with him. Believing in him for true forgiveness of your sins and accepting his gift of grace for salvation. An everlasting life with him, not apart from him."

"Jesus, please go. Go away. I want to be alone now." I push Jesus back with words. If I never see him again, that will be all right with me.

"Okay, I will go. But, Seth, your father is right. Following the law by itself will not make you happy. God doesn't want you to be this great religious person who knows all about his teachings and strives to work for his pardon. He simply wants you to believe and trust in him. Many of the religious leaders and priests sitting around the temple courtyard know about God. They can quote scripture after scripture, and talk about the laws handed down, but they truly don't know him. God wants you to know him, not just *about* Him. And your father is right again when he says a person can't do enough or be good enough. That's why I am standing right here in front of you now. You won't understand what I just said, but soon, very soon, I will tell you more about how all your 'do enoughs' and 'good enoughs' will be provided for."

Jesus turns and walks away. I stand there in the doorway, watching him get smaller and smaller in the distance. What was Jesus talking about?

Little did I know then that we wouldn't speak to each other again for more than eighteen years.

Part Two   Beyond Enough

Chapter Twelve

Seth

I hope I can get through the day with no mention of what this day marks. When I was twelve, it was fun. Not now. I hate this day.

I walk past the small table and chair Mother uses to brush her hair and catch a glimpse of my reflection in her round, silver-backed mirror. The swirly decorations make it look like an item only a woman would want. I pick up the mirror and raise it to my face. My beard is the longest it has ever been. I can see streaks of gray running through it. It may be only my thirtieth birthday, but I look like my old man, which I hate. I may have his ways, but I didn't want his gray hair.

For the past eighteen years, I've been on the road almost every week stealing and conning people out of their hard-earned money. That can take a toll on one's body and soul. Those are just two of the reasons I am still single, using my parent's home as a base. I don't want to get married right now. It's not a good life to give a wife. I know because I saw it with my own eyes. What if I have children? Would I be able to throw away the family whip, never to strike the back of an innocent child? Or would I be like all the past fathers of the family? Perhaps the only way I can show love to a child is not to have one.

Lately, when I return home from a trip, Mother is more likely to bring up the subjects of settling down with a wife and giving her grandchildren to spoil. Heaven knows I wasn't spoiled when I was a child. I tend to like the life we have now. With the help of other people's money and possessions, we can now afford nicer things. I like the bigger house, the nicer clothes, and all the sheep and goats that fill the field. Of course, there is also the sound of gold and silver clanging together in my leather pouch. But most of all, I prefer to have different women in different towns.

Upon that subject, my thoughts immediately turn to one woman who might be able to change my mind. Unfortunately, I am just one of her gentleman friends. Recently, I have been finding every excuse possible to travel near her town of Sychar so I can stop by and see her. She might be that someone special for me. Then again, probably not.

I hear the back door open and recognize a voice I never tire of hearing.

"Seth, Seth, are you still here? Come quick into the kitchen!"

I lay the mirror back on the table and head toward the voice. I'm not looking forward to putting on a happy face.

"Yes, Mother, I'm coming."

I enter the kitchen and see Mother holding a new leather pouch with my name engraved in the leather.

She is so excited. "Seth, here," she says, "I wanted to give this to you before you leave again."

Mother hands me the beautiful leather pouch and then reaches up on the tip of her toes to wrap her arms around my neck. As she settles back on her feet, I say, "Thank you. It's beautiful." I manage an authentic grin of pleasure.

Putting the pouch up to my nose I take in the fresh smell of new leather. It's a different smell from the leather whip that has been worn, used, and stained with blood.

"It smells so good. I will never let it out of my sight. Wherever it goes with me you will be right by my side." I give her another hug before telling her, "I must go and pack now."

"Where to this time?"

"Bethany."

"What's going on there?"

"Well, this man called John the Baptizer preaches to large crowds about a coming messiah. The political leaders are getting agitated at him for the message he is spewing. I couldn't care less about his sermons, but many people gather to hear what he is selling. This will be a great time for me and Father to work the crowd and pick the pouches of many who will be watching him and not us."

"Seth, don't tell me anymore." Mother covers her ears.

"Have you ever thought about doing something else? Thirty is not too old to start over, you know." She gives me a look that a son can't ignore.

"As long as you have breath you have time. You have some money now. There is enough livestock to split with you. I think you would make a great livestock farmer. You could work here and we wouldn't have to pay a herdsman." Mother grabs my arm as if to say, "Please don't go."

"No." I break her hold on me and move away. "The only thing I know about livestock is how to eat it. I do what I do because I want to. I like it to the point I don't think I could change my life even if I wanted to."

She moves in front of me to block my exit. "Seth," she says, "That's not true. Anybody can change the path of their life. It might not be easy, but it can be done. Maybe you should ask God to help you."

"Ask God! What God? Mother, has Jesus' mother been putting crazy ideas about a god in your head? You'd better not let Father hear you talk like this. He would be furious, and there's no telling what that crazy old man would do to you." I point behind me as if he might be there.

Mother points her thumb at her collarbone. "Mary has shared some things about God with me, that's all. No one is persuading me to believe in something or someone I don't want to. I can think for myself."

"You have Father telling you, no, *demanding* there will be no real religion in our family—only the outside appearance so we can do business with rich Jews. Now you have Mary telling you about some God who deserves your loyalty. Which person is it smarter for you to side with? Someone is going to convince you to one side or the other."

Folding her arms, she says, "You're right. Someone will, and at this moment God is winning." With tears falling from her eyes, Mother turns and walks out of the kitchen, out of the house.

Chapter Thirteen

I feel bad about making Mother cry on my birthday. That's the last thing I want to do. I know she loves me and only wants the best for me. But right now, I only want the best from the people gathered in Bethany: their best jewelry, gold, silver, money, whatever they have for the picking.

Father and I throw our packs on the back of our newest business acquisition. It's a young donkey I call Able. He is more "Able" than I to carry out newfound possessions. Father calls him something else . . . I like my name better. I appreciate the sacrifice this poor animal is making for us. Father couldn't care less.

As we approach the town, we see hundreds of people—maybe even more—making their way to the bank of the Jordan River. Voices fill the air with excitement. Some shout, "Baptizer! Immerse me in the water!"

With all these people crammed together on this hot day, a light breeze whisks the stench of human body odor across the air. It does nothing more than remind us of the need for a dip in the water. I might be willing to be dunked for a quick relief from the sun. I tug on Able's rope to keep him moving so he doesn't stop and rest. If he stops, I probably will not get this beast moving again for another day or two.

As Father and I reach the rim of the river, we can see that this stretch of water sits down in a valley hemmed in by two banks. It's the perfect bowl shape for John the Baptizer to lead people into the waist-deep water for their cleansing. Hundreds of people are already gathered, sitting along the bank as if this had been designed and built for this occasion.

A man stands thigh-high in the waters of the Jordan. His long, matted hair hangs below his shoulders; his long beard flies in every direction as the wind gently passes. His clothes look like the skins of the animals he must live with in the wilderness: wild and woolly. I'm sure he probably smells like them too. The man looks exactly like what they call him: the wild man preacher of the wilderness.

The wild man is preaching. His hand is in the air, pounding the sky. His voice bellows to all who came to see and hear.

"Repent!" he shouts. "For the kingdom of heaven is near."

I look at Father, he looks at me, and we both laugh. Father mocks them by saying, "If this is heaven, you can keep it. There are too many of *those people* here for me to want to stay."

Those people are the religious fanatics, as Father calls them. He hates them.

As if the wild man hears my father, he looks right up in our direction and says, "You don't care about what God has for you. A simple baptism in this river water won't change you. No, your life must change. Your heart must change. If you truly want to live a life that honors God, get in line to be baptized. If not, step aside and let the ones who do take your place."

As the wild man reaches for the next person in line, a voice behind where Father and I are standing says, "I do. I want to be baptized."

Like the old story about the Red Sea, the crowd parts, leaving a gap that leads to the river. A man walks along the newly created path. I look at him and then do a double-take. He looks familiar, though I'm not sure where I've seen him before. Father tugs on my robe sleeve and says, "Look, Seth, that is the boy named Jesus from Nazareth. You used to play together when you were kids."

"How do you know it's Jesus?" I ask.

The man is tall, and lean. He's wearing a long white robe. His hair is long, and so is his beard.

"Seth, I ran into him about a month ago in Nazareth. At the marketplace. He was shopping for his mother while I was shoplifting, as usual, for your mother. Jesus asked about you, wanted to know how you were doing."

It hits me. I haven't seen Jesus for some eighteen years since I told him to leave the house. Then shortly after that, Father bought land for our expanding livestock. The acres are about a half-day's journey outside of Nazareth. He built a larger house for Mother in hopes that it would remove the strain of their on-again, off-again relationship. For the most part, it just gave them more room to fight.

For a split second, I close my eyes and see Jesus as the twelve-year-old boy I remember, not the thirty-year-old man he is today. He was true to his word, honoring my demand to never come round again.

As Jesus walks past, he's about twenty feet away from me. We make eye contact, his seems to say, "It's good to see an old friend." He then nods his head and walks on.

As Jesus makes his way down the path toward the water's edge, the wild man walks toward the riverbank, drops to his knees, and says, "I can't baptize you. I am the one who should be baptized by you. I'm not worthy to wear your sandals, let alone baptize you."

Jesus stands before the wild man, John the Baptizer, who is now crying. Jesus reaches down and helps John back up on his feet.

"John, you must baptize me. The time has come for me to begin my journey on this earth. My journey is to tell people what my true purpose is."

With tears streaming down his cheeks, the baptizer takes Jesus by the hand and turns toward the river. The pair walk into the water. The hundreds of people watching are silent, taking in all they see. Not a sound is heard other than the soft, smooth stream of fresh water flowing onto the river's edge. The still water has now come to life.

The baptizer places his left arm around Jesus' shoulders and then raises his right hand to the sky. As the wild man looks into the clouds, his lips move, though only Jesus can hear. In a few moments, his lips stop moving. He then lowers his right hand to gently lay Jesus down into the water. Jesus' head disappears underwater for a quick moment.

Immediately after he comes out of the water, the clouds separate. Many people gasp in awe. I, too, sense this moment is amazing.

Jesus reaches up to the sky with both arms as if he is trying to grab someone or something. Father and I glance at each other, not knowing what to say. Then Jesus shouts, "Yes! I see the spirit of God, the kingdom of heaven. This is what it is all about."

Jesus says more, speaking upward as if he is talking to someone, but I can't hear him this time. He appears to be experiencing great wonderment and joy.

Jesus and John walk out of the river side by side with their arms draped over each other's shoulders. Their smiles are as wide as the Jordan River.

Father moves closer to me and says, "So I guess Jesus is perfect now. He's been dunked in the water. If that is all it takes, I might have to go jump in myself."

Without saying a word, I turn and walk up the hill. What did Jesus mean when he said, "I see the Spirit of God. This is what it is all about. It is time for me to start telling people about my true purpose?"

What is Jesus talking about? Do I want to know? Back to reality, I do know I need to get to work with Father. There's too much opportunity here for us to miss. Now I regret I wasn't working the crowd while they were watching Jesus get wet. There's no telling how much we could have made off the gawkers. Oh well, I won't miss the next great opportunity. Maybe all Father and I should do is follow Jesus to the next big religious spectacle.

Chapter Fourteen

Seth

Finally, we're back in Nazareth. Father and I have counted all the loot we got in Bethany. Not a bad take for the few days of conning the gullible people traveling for the great baptisms. Who knew so many would pay to be baptized in the *magical waters* of the Jordan River? I also did a little pickpocketing and lightened the load of more than one donkey. Father played the part of a preacher from the hill country quite convincingly. I deceived them out of their money and Father dunked them out of their guilt.

After about the eightieth baptism, some did realize we weren't very holy. We barely escaped from the mob and made it out alive. I'm not sure, but I think the Roman guards also searched for us. We're going to lie low for a while at home. It's good to sleep in my own bed, and, of course, eat Mother's great cooking.

After waiting at home for more than two months, Father and I decided it was time to sell some of the stolen possessions we acquired. I know Mother is about to go crazy with us both being home longer than usual. Father is the one she can do without most days. Me, she likes having home more as long as I don't sleep all day and get in the way of the servants working around the house.

I thought the time together might offer some great father-son time. We could create special moments like the time at the pond or have meaningful conversations that would never leave my memory. But no. The only special moments during those two months were when he didn't hurl insults at me or cause Mother to run off crying after his vulgar words sliced through her and stripped away any feelings of self-worth she might still be clinging to. Not that he needed any help to be mean, but the strong drink he chugged down most days sure didn't help. Mother and I would take turns hiding the bottles his so-called friends would drop off. After about four days of that, we discovered his friends were bringing two bottles. One for the hide-and-seek we were playing and one for the hide-and-drink father was playing.

Time finally came for Father and I to say goodbye to Mother. We leave the house and walk past the local synagogue. As I walk by a small window, I see Jesus seated in the middle of the young priests.

I grab Father's arm to show that I want to linger and watch what is going on with Jesus. We enter the synagogue and stand behind the crowd now gathered around Jesus. I wonder why so many want to gather around him, and then I realize that I do the same thing. *Why?*

Just as we get settled, Jesus says, "The Spirit of the Lord is on me. I am the one preaching the good news. I am the one the Father has sent to you."

A voice rings out next to my ear. The words cause me to jump because I'm not expecting anyone to disrupt Jesus, especially not my father. "Hey!" he shouts. "Isn't this guy none other than the son of Joseph the carpenter? The snot-nosed, pesky kid who grew up right here in town? My son grew up with him."

When Father mentions my role in this, I shrug back farther from the crowd, not wanting to be seen.

Father can't take a hint. He yells to the crowd, "Are you going to let him tell you he is some kind of chosen one? Maybe Jesus should go elsewhere and spout his teachings. Do you priests really want him meddling in your synagogue?

He's coming in here and talking as if he's a know-it-all prophet. That's hard to take."

I can't believe Father is saying all this. Others in the crowd now speak up: "Yes, he is a nobody."

Another person shouts, "Aran is right. We shouldn't listen to his nonsense. Jesus should leave our town."

Looking through the maze of heads in front of me, I see Jesus stand up. He holds up his right hand and calmly says, "Very well, I will leave. It is true that a prophet is never accepted by those closest to him. I am indeed a carpenter's son, and I have played with many of your kids growing up. But I am more than the kid down the street who grew tall. I am the truth." He looks at the leaders in the synagogue. "The scriptures you have read, studied, and taught for many generations are being fulfilled today."

Then Jesus scans the room and makes eye contact with many. He steps backward to show he's leaving, but he closes his sermon with, "The truth is standing right here in front of you, and you still can't see the way. From this day forward, you have heard the good news. What you do with it is up to you. But know God's grace is for all who seek it."

Jesus isn't moving fast enough for the rowdy crowd who want him gone. They close in around him.

A voice shouts from the middle of the crowd. "Grab him!"

Someone else shouts, "I've got him!"

My father yells, "Let's show him who the true prophets of this town are."

The mob separates, and so I get a glimpse of Jesus being held captive.

But the three men holding their prey look at one another with confused expressions. They don't have Jesus at all. No, they've hauled off a husky, older woman, who just happens to sell the best oat cookies in the marketplace. I know this because Jesus and I would go to her booth to get a cookie or two. We loved them. She loved us. Most times she would give the cookies to us for free. I didn't even have to steal them.

The cookie lady shakes herself free of the men. "Why did you do that?" she yells. "You made me drop my sack of cookies. I brought them for Jesus."

In all the fuss and confusion, I look to see where Jesus is. He is gone. I certainly will not say it out loud, but I am kind of glad he got away.

During the entire trip back to the house after we cashed in our loot, Father complains about what Jesus said. "How dare he think of himself as a prophet! Then he tells us he has some kind of good news for us. The *real* good news is he is gone. He'd better not come back to Nazareth."

I remain silent, but all the while I keep playing in my mind, *what did Jesus mean when he said he was the truth; I am the one the Father has sent?* Why would his father, the town carpenter, send him out? Out where? For what?

Maybe Jesus is crazy like my father thinks he is. Jesus was always different from my other friends growing up. Yes, a little preachy at times, but you always knew he cared about you.

Chapter Fifteen

Naomi

As the servant finishes up the dishes from the day's meals, I sit down at my small table tucked in the corner of my chamber. This is one of my favorite places to go when I want some quiet time alone. My two most prized possessions sit on the table. My grandmother gave them to me on my wedding day. One is a beautiful horsehair brush with a bronze handle. A mirror with an ornate, silver handle always sits beside it. I realize having them is a privilege. Valuable and beautiful items like these are usually owned only by women of wealthy families.

My grandmother, not a wealthy woman herself, told me she got them from someone special and wanted me to have them since I was someone special to her. I always knew I was her favorite grandchild. She is the only other person besides Mary who told me about God. She would say to me, "It is always better to give than receive. You can't out-give God. God's blessings are pressed down and poured out to all who will stretch out their open hands to him."

I didn't understand what she was saying half the time, but I knew she believed in what she was saying. To this day, I don't think someone gave the mirror and brush to her. My heart tells me she spent what little money she had hidden away and borrowed the rest to buy them for me. Her generosity is the only thing I treasure from my wedding day.

With each stroke of the brush going through my long,

black hair, my mind takes me to beautiful worlds I have never seen but can imagine. Seth comes into the room, startling me back to the real world. Without missing a beat, he tells me about his day with Aran at the synagogue.

Sensing he wants my full attention, I put the hairbrush down. "Grab a chair," I say, "and join me at the table."

"You should have heard what Jesus was telling the priests at the synagogue. He was proclaiming to be a prophet, telling the crowd that he was 'the truth.' He says his father sent him to tell all who will listen about the good news. Can you believe it? He's crazy, isn't he? A lot of people listening thought so. They wanted to throw him out of town. I thought they were going to hurt him. That was one angry mob."

I feel my face flush, and without a second thought, I throw my hairbrush on the table with enough force everything resting on top takes a bounce. "I don't think Jesus is crazy," I counter. "Just because we don't understand all he is telling people since his return from Bethany doesn't automatically make him crazy."

A little embarrassed, I lean forward and straighten up the toppled items on top of my table.
"What if he's telling the truth?" I say, my back now to Seth. "Maybe he has been chosen to tell us about God and about how we should live. Haven't you ever thought there might be more to life than the one here on earth? Life here can get messy. If there is a real heaven, wouldn't it be great to go there one day?"

Seth seems taken aback and asks, "You don't believe in all that religious stuff, do you? That there is a God, a heaven?"

"I don't know what I believe at this moment of my life. But I am going to keep searching for answers." I prop my elbows on the table and rest my face in my hands. "Please don't tell your father. You know what he thinks, and he doesn't want anyone else thinking any different from what he does."

Seth places his hand on my shoulder. "I won't tell Father. For me, I'm going to keep on living my life as I want to. Living day by day, doing what makes me feel happy. I'm creating my own heaven on earth. That's what Father believes, and for once, I agree with him."

He stands and pats my shoulder for a time or two. "One thing I do know, you're not crazy, Mother. Love you."

He steps out, leaving me where he found me. I fold my arms on top of the table and lay my head down. Closing my eyes, I drift off to sleep.

After what seems to be only minutes, I awake with one arm stretched out as far as it will go and the other draped over it. I hear the clatter of pans as one of the servants works in the kitchen. It's the start of a new day.

Still thinking about the conversation I had with Seth last night, I've got some questions, and I want to find answers. I decide to visit Mary.

It's a beautiful morning for a walk. The sky is blue without a cloud in it. It's not too far of a walk—a mile or two—but I want to go and get back before the midday sun heats up. Plus, I need to get back home before Aran discovers I'm gone and asks where I've been.

I hope Mary won't mind my showing up at her door unexpectedly. I approach the small, modest house. I'm not even sure she'll be at home. Nervously, I knock on the front door.

The door flies open, and Mary greets me with a smile as bright as the morning sun. "Naomi!" she speaks my name with a voice full of joy.

"What a great surprise to see you. Please come in." Mary steps back from the door and makes room for me to step inside.

"Thanks, Mary," I say. I can't match her enthusiasm because I'm still worried I'm intruding. "I hope you don't mind my barging in on you like this."

"Oh no, I am so glad you're here. It's been a while since

we got together. Let's talk in the sitting room by the fire. We will have a hot drink. I have a pot already made. I must have known you were going to stop by today."

Sitting next to the warm fire helps me calm down and gather my thoughts. I sip my drink to give me time to think about what I want to discuss. I must have given away that I have something on my mind because Mary asks, "Naomi, is everything okay? It looks to me as if you might be struggling with something."

I shake my head. "No, there's nothing bad going on. But I have come here to ask you some questions."

"Okay, fire away. I'll try to answer if I can."

I pause for a second and take another sip. Trying to think of how to start, I decide to be blunt. "Tell me about Jesus."

There's a silence, an awkward silence. And I realize I need to share some gossip. "There are a lot of people talking about what Jesus has been sharing at the synagogue since his return from Bethany. They say Jesus claims to be a prophet sent from God to share what he calls good news."

I pull my cup closer to my face as if I am trying to hide behind it. "My husband told me some want to run him out of town because of what he is saying. Even a few of the high priests are angry at what Jesus is telling people." I take a longer sip this time.

"Naomi, I will tell you all. But you won't fully understand everything I tell you."

I let that odd comment settle, and I nod to encourage her to continue, wrapping my hands around the cup.

Mary leans forward. "Jesus will say and do things that will not be fully understood. But soon, it will be made clear."

Mary leans back and presses her fingertips together. "Okay, where do I start? Jesus' existence is not typical. Yes, I am his mother here on earth, and yes, Joseph was his father here on earth, but Jesus was sent here by his heavenly Father to give us something we can never earn or deserve. He is the way, the truth, the light, and everlasting life. Jesus is a gift from God. God loves you, me, and everyone so much he gave us Jesus, and if we believe in him, we will have eternal life with him in his heavenly kingdom."

I doubt Jesus can love Aran, but I have hope for Seth. "Do you mean everyone includes people like my husband and Seth, people who do bad things? Those who steal and hurt people to get what they want no matter how it affects others? Those who only care about themselves?"

Mary smiles as if I've given her a present. "Naomi, no one is ever going to be good enough to get to heaven. That's why God sent Jesus so everyone, including your husband and Seth, can have salvation and eternal life in heaven. But anyone who wants that must believe that Jesus is who he says he is. We must trust in him. It's like dying to yourself, not living a selfish life all about you, but living a life honoring him, seeking his desire for your life. Our true purpose in life, no matter who we are or what we do, is to know, love, and accept Jesus as our Lord and Savior, and then go tell others."

My head is swirling with all kinds of thoughts. I asked Mary to tell me about Jesus, and boy did she. I'm still not sure what to think. Mary's revelations are overwhelming.

"Mary, I think I should be going. Thank you for the drink. The figs add great flavor to it. I will have to try that at home." I place the cup down on a small table next to the hearth and stand up. "I have taken a lot of your time this morning. My husband is going to be wondering where I am, anxious for me to get back and fix him something to eat. I do think there is something special about Jesus. I know he tried to help Seth when they were kids. I appreciate that very much. Maybe Jesus and Seth will run into each other again someday and Jesus can help Seth get his life on the right path."

The fire crackles and hisses as I leave the room and exit the house. During the entire walk home, I can't stop thinking about what Mary told me about Jesus. I certainly don't fully understand everything. I hope it will be made clearer soon. Right now, soon can't come soon enough.

Chapter Sixteen

Seth

I'm on the road again. Father suggested we divide and conquer so he went his way, and I am going my way. My first destination is Cana of Galilee, about eight miles from home. I have the great joy of attending a friend's wedding. I'm not excited about going, but I am looking forward to a party with lots of food and wine.

After a short overnight stay in Cana, I will then head to Sychar where my girlfriend lives. I wish she could have joined me in Cana for the marriage ceremony. I miss her. She also likes a good party.

It's been way too long since we've seen each other. Father says he likes her a lot because "she's tough, and she likes to live life fast and free. She's the opposite of your mother who is straight and steady—boring."

I have to remind myself this first part of my trip is not business as usual but pleasure. My friend Nathanael is getting married. When we were around twelve, I remember swimming at the pond with Jesus and some of the other boys in town. We would take turns carrying one another on our shoulders, one pair wrestling the other to see who could throw the others off. We'd yell victoriously with hands stretched to the sky, ready for another battle.

One day I hoisted Nathanael on my shoulders for the next match when we heard mysterious giggles coming from a patch of bushes near the edge of the pond. Through the thin branches, I could make out at least three girls hunched down trying to watch Nathanael be the victor. I knew he was the favored because Ruth would tell me all the girls liked him. Why not? He had the looks that turned heads. He had a tutor, so he was better educated than the rest of us, and he came from a wealthy family.

Like me, he worked for his father. Only his father's business was legitimate. He had a lot of land and raised camels, horses, and cattle between Nazareth and the Kishon River. His father's business had expanded from Nazareth to Cana, and so his parents had moved to Cana, leaving Nathanael in Nazareth.

Nathanael always said he couldn't wait to escape from Nazareth when he was old enough to leave. I'm not sure why, but he just didn't like living there.

Nathanael's escape is coming true today. His father wants him to join him in Cana. He's no longer needed to oversee the business from Nazareth. He's taking Sarah along with him. She is one of those girls who was hiding behind the bushes. They are to be married at his parents' home in Cana. Nathanael shared with me the last time we talked over a goblet of wine that her parents agreed to his father hosting. Their status in life was nowhere near their future son-in-law's. And they didn't mind latching on to Nathanael's parents' robe tails.

So, I imagine when his father told him to come to Cana and he would host their marriage ceremony, Nathanael and his future in-laws probably couldn't say yes fast enough.

His father is known for hosting some impressive parties; he serves the best food and wine money can buy. He has the reputation of sparing no expense when it comes to throwing a party. Since I hate going to Jewish wedding ceremonies, I love to hear at least the celebration feast will be worth attending.

My three-hour journey is coming to an end. I see the

grand marble steps leading up to two wood-carved doors placed perfectly behind stone columns lining the front of this magnificent house.

Wow, what a property! I haven't ever been in a house like this before. No wonder Nathanael wants his wedding here. Maybe I will be able to have a mansion like this someday. All around the massive rooms are fine linens hanging from the windows and beautiful furniture lining the walls. The spread of food placed on pristine silver platters seems to go on forever. There's a small band of musicians playing softly in the corner.

Thirsty from my trip, I head to the large cisterns and get a glass of wine. Then I wander around, looking at all the finery.

I am standing in awe of the gorgeous paintings of Jerusalem in the glory days. I am taking it all in when I feel a tap on my right shoulder. I turn, and to my surprise, none other than Jesus himself is standing next to me. A grin grows from side to side on his face. "Seth," he says, "it's certainly good to see you. How are you?"

With an awkward laugh, I say, "Man, did you ever think Sarah would be the one to snatch up Nathanael? So much for prearranged marriages. I guess true love won over bride price and position."

"Yes, Mother and I were talking on our trip here. Sarah will make a good wife. Out of all the Nazarene girls, she always seemed to be the best match for him. He needed to see the other side of living—the simple life of modest means, not just the life of luxury and wealth.

She will be good for his parents too."

His smile turns serious as he asks, "So, Seth how's your love life? Any plans of getting married soon? Don't keep your . . . *girlfriend* waiting too long."

How does Jesus know about Tabitha? Does he know our true relationship? I want to change the subject, and fast. I take a big sip of my wine to collect my thoughts. "I hear you're like me," I say, "doing a lot of traveling."

"Yes. I'll be going through Samaria in the next couple of days," Jesus replies.

I have to sidestep so some of the servants can pass between us. The trays the servants are carrying give me a chance to change the subject. "Look at that food! Nathanael's folks sure know how to host a wedding feast. Have you tried the lamb?"

"No, not yet," Jesus says. Then, like a dog with a bone, he goes back to the subject I want to avoid. "What will you be doing in Samaria?"

"I've got some business to do there. My father is there now waiting for me. Hey, I am sorry about how he treated you back in Nazareth a couple of weeks ago."

"It's okay. I know many people won't understand what I'm doing. That's why I must keep moving forward, sharing the Good News with as many people as possible. It's even time for me to step it up more."

Mary comes walking toward us. "Seth! I didn't know you were here!" she says. "It's so good to see you. Is your mother here too?"

"No, she couldn't come. She's not feeling well."

It's not that she was ill, but just uncharacteristically melancholy and pensive. My guess from talking to Mary about God too much.

"Plus, I'm traveling on to Capernaum after the reception. Mother didn't want to have to travel back home by herself." That part I know is true.

Mary now seems pensive herself. "I'm sorry she isn't feeling well," she says. "I'll check in on her when I get back home." Her manner seems preoccupied, and she forces a smile.

"Seth, excuse me, but I need to talk to Jesus in private for a moment."

Jesus and Mary walk toward three floor-to-ceiling marble columns with beautiful fabric draped from their tops.

The fabric swoops down to mid-height and then back up again to the next column. The fabric looks as if it came from Asia. Nathanael's father trades expensive horses that are bred for desert travel in exchange for special, hard-to-acquire goods.

Being nosey, I watch from behind a column off to the side of the room. I'm at a good vantage point to watch Mary and Jesus. She whispers something near Jesus' left ear. As soon as she is done, Jesus takes a half step back and lifts his right arm indicating some type of frustration, as if he isn't too pleased with what his mother has to say. But not another word is said, and Mary walks away.

Well, I guess that's over. I need another glass of wine.

I step away from the column I was snooping behind and walk toward a table centered between two windows at the south end of the massive room.

Mary talks to one of the servants. I stop behind her to wait for a refill of my cup, when I hear her say to the servant, "Whatever Jesus tells you, do it."

She steps away. Now it's my turn to get some more wine, but to my surprise, the server tells me there is no more.

"What! There's no more wine? You have to be joking," I complain to the server, wanting to reveal that's the main reason I'm even here, but I keep that inside.

I'm not easily separated from getting a drink, and I wonder if the servant just doesn't want to serve me. "How about those six pots over there," I say, pointing behind the columns. "What's in those?" They were big enough to hold twenty to thirty gallons each.

"They are empty, sir."

About this time Jesus puts his hand on my shoulder, indicating for me to step aside. I do.

Jesus says with a firm but respectful tone, "Take these six water pots and fill them to the very top with water. After you are done, take them to the host of this reception."

Water? I don't want a cup of water. There's got to be

more wine, or I'm out of here. Okay, so I begin to say my goodbyes, tell people it was good to see them, it was a great wedding. I'm forcing my last farewell smile when I notice one of the six large water pots is being placed by the wedding couple and their parents.

Nathanael dips his cup into one of the six water pots. He looks inside his cup with an expression of surprise. He swirls whatever is in his cup, sniffs it, then takes a sip. His eyes open wide, he leans forward, quickly talks to the servant, and then turns to the crowd and shouts, "Wine! There is more wine. Come and get it!"

Wine! How can that be? Jesus told them to fill the pots with water. How can the water now be wine? I have to see and taste it for myself. I run over to the nearest pot, dip my empty cup into it, and drink as if I haven't had a drink in forty days. To my pleasant surprise, it tastes like wine, real wine, not water.

Let the party go on! Wow! This is the best wine I have ever tasted. I grab one of the server's arms as he is walking by. "Hey," I whisper. "Tell me, how did you get this great wine so fast? No way you could have gone into town and bought this wine. Plus, no one serves wine as good as this."

"Sir, I am telling you the truth," he answers. "We did as the man Jesus told us to do. We took the six water pots, filled them with water, and brought them straight back to the host. The water became the wine. That's what you're now drinking. It's a miracle if I ever saw one, and I haven't, until now."

No way! Jesus turned those pots of water into wine. How can he have done that? How can anyone do that?

Chapter Seventeen

Seth

Is the ceiling spinning out of control? Or is my head fighting a war with the wine? I have never drank that much wine before. Placing my hands on both sides of my head, I shout, "Stop! Please stop spinning! I'm going to be sick."

Yes, that was a prediction. Sick I got—all over my feet and sleep mat. Lying back down, I watch the spinning ceiling slowly come to a stop, and I realize I have overslept. The way I feel at this moment, I'm not sure I can start my thirty-mile trek to Sychar. That will not be good. This time two people will be mad at me—Father and my girlfriend. She knew I was coming right after the wedding feast. She will be expecting me to be on time, her time.

I hate to admit it, but this thirty-year-old man with sick sticking to his feet is a bit afraid of both of them. I feel miserable, but that wine was sure the best I've ever had. It is worth the trouble I'm in for being late. I'm going from the best wine ever to the biggest whine of my father and girlfriend. That thought makes me laugh.

I finally made it to my girlfriend's house a day and a half late. And it's perfect timing too. It's midday, getting hotter by the minute, and my appetite has returned from the overindulgence of two days ago. Yes, I'm hungry.

I knock on her door. Nothing. No one seems to be home. I go ahead and push open the door, and then I poke my head inside. Yes, the house is empty. One of her water jugs and some fruits are sitting in the middle of a table. Water and a piece of fruit will be great. It should hold me over until she returns.

I drop my travel bag in the back corner of the room and walk over to the table sitting in the middle of the small, one-room house. I pick up the water jug, and to my disappointment, it is empty. A quick thought crosses my mind: *Where's Jesus when you need him*? It doesn't even have to be wine. A tall mug of water would bring life to this hot, dry, dead-feeling body of mine. I guess I will just lie down on my bed mat and take a nap until she returns. I unroll my mat and place it against the wall opposite the door.

I fall into a deep, peaceful sleep when suddenly a loud bang rings out, startling me awake. The wall I'm leaning against shakes like the whole house is falling on me. I rise, ready to run for my life when I see Tabitha coming in through the door. She almost falls on her face because she is moving so fast.

"Seth! Seth!" she shouts. "Get up! I have to tell you what just happened to me! You won't believe it!"

"Okay, okay! Settle down," I say. "Here, sit down. Catch your breath."

I grab a chair and place it under her. Pulling up another chair I sit beside her.

I hold her hands in mine, hoping she will calm down enough to tell me what happened. Selfishly I'm also hoping her story will overshadow my being a day and a half late.

"Seth, I went up to the well to get water as I usually do this time of day. As I have told you before, the women look down their noses at me. The life I live isn't as pure or perfect as they think theirs is. I'm too worldly for them. You know, I'm the wild girl in town. With all the husbands and boyfriends I've had, I'm trash to them."

I squeeze her hand and say, "I hate that the other women make you feel the way you do. You shouldn't have to get your water in the hottest part of the day. I've told you before, don't worry about what they think. I think you are perfect."

"But it was different today," Tabitha says. "Something amazing happened to me."

Her face glows as she continues with the story. "I had just got the heavy jug filled with water up to the rim of the well when I heard this voice from behind me say, 'Would you give me a drink of water?' I jumped, startled, almost dropping my water jug down the well. I turned around and saw this man sitting on the ground. He was leaning up against a tree with his sandals off lying next to him. He realized he scared me and said, 'Sorry. I didn't mean to scare you like that.'

"Trying to catch my breath I said, 'I didn't see you there. I'm usually the only one here this time of day.' He said, 'Yes, I understand. It's tough being around women who like to point fingers and talk bad about others when they have enough of their own issues to deal with. No one is without sin. Shame on them.'"

"Seth, I then realize this man is a Jew. They don't like people like me. Samaritans and Jews don't chit-chat together. As one Jew once told me, 'I wouldn't be caught dead talking to you or any other Samaritan,' and then he spat on the ground right next to my foot."

Rubbing her hands gently, I say, "Honey, it's a good thing I wasn't around when that happened. I would have corrected his prejudiced thinking with a fist or two against his face."

She smiles. "Yes, I know you would have come to my rescue, but quiet, let me talk, there's lots more to tell you. Okay, so then I said to the man, 'You don't know what I am? People like you and me don't sit around the watering hole swapping stories. No, we're to despise each other. You know, for no other reason than you are you and I'm me. Are we really that different from each other? We don't look that different from one another. Some of us Samaritans might be a little darker than some of you Jews. I look like this, whatever that is, and you look like you look, whatever that is. Wow, now that is a good reason, right? If others walked up this hill and saw us talking together, probably both of us would be strung up that tall tree you're leaning against.

"Then he cleared his throat and said, 'So, does this mean you won't give me a sip of that cold water you are desperately clinging on to? If only you knew who I truly am . . . you would be asking me for a drink of water.' So, I placed the jug down next to me."

A grin grows across my face. "Honey, I can see you throwing your hip out to one side, placing your hand on it as if to say, 'Who do you think you are?'"

"Don't laugh. Yes, I'm a little ticked at his arrogance in thinking I would want a drink from him. I thought, how are going to give me a drink when you don't even have anything to dip the water out with?"

"This man then chuckled and said, 'Yes, you're right. My arms aren't long enough for my hands to scoop out a drink. But I will tell you this: Everyone who drinks out of that well will get thirsty again and again. Anyone who drinks the water I give will never thirst again, not ever again. The water I give gushes fountains of endless life."

She puts her hands together. "He cupped his hands together like this as if he was holding water. Then water dripped from his clasped hands. It overflowed the top and soaked the dry ground, turning it to mud."

I jump in and ask, "Why didn't you just get your water and leave? Why did you keep talking to this crazy man who was doing some kind of magic trick to impress you?"

Now Tabitha bounced back and forth on her feet, excited. "No, Seth, it wasn't any kind of trick. I know because I was there standing right in front of him."

She plants herself right in front of me. "There was no trick going on," she says. "The water overflowing from this man's hands was real. It gets really real next."

I raise an eyebrow as she continues. "I stared at his hands which were flooded with clear water. 'Sir,' I said, 'give me this water so I won't ever get thirsty, won't ever have to come back to this well again.'"

She looks at me, her expression full of rapture. "Now get ready for what's next! The man said, 'Go call your husband and then come back.' I told him I didn't have a husband. He said, 'That's nicely put: I have no husband. You've had five husbands, and the man you live with now isn't even your husband. You spoke the truth there, sure enough.'"

She rocks back and turns away from me. A moment later turns back around and throws her arms up in the air. Guilty on all accounts.

"I was taken aback by his knowing all about my personal life, so I said, 'Oh, so you're a prophet! Tell me this—my people worshiped God at this mountain, but the Jews say that Jerusalem is the only place for worship, is that right?' He looked straight into my eyes and said, 'Woman a time is coming, soon, matter of fact, it's here now, where it won't matter where you worship, or what you are called. It's who you are and the way you live that count before God. True worshipers will worship the Father in spirit and truth. That's the kind of worshiper the Father seeks." Tabitha folds her arms in front of her.

I reach out and say, "It's okay if you're frustrated or confused, that guy told you a lot of stuff. I probably would have reacted the same way."

I'm not sure what to say, but I try to be the good boyfriend and console her.

She rests her arms on my shoulders. "Thanks for listening. Even though I didn't grow up in a religious family, my grandfather sometimes talked about the old Scripture writings of a coming Messiah. Grandfather said the Messiah would be called Christ. Remembering this, I told the man, 'Well, when the Messiah they call Christ comes, he will explain everything to us.' Then the last thing the man said to me was 'I, Jesus, who speaks to you, am he. You don't have to wait any longer or look any further.'"

I jump from my chair, knocking it over. Her arms go flying off my shoulders.

"Jesus!" I shout. "This man told you he was Jesus?"

Tabitha seems shocked at my outburst. "What's wrong?" she asks. "Do you know this man named Jesus?"

"Yes. I know a man named Jesus, a religious sort. He goes around talking like a prophet. He supposedly turned water into wine at the wedding I just attended."

"Seth, I'm sure this is the same Jesus. But talking to him did something to me. I feel like a different person now. You must go and see him for yourself. Talk to him."

I just looked down at the floor, sad for Tabitha. "No thanks. I'm fine just the way I am."

She seems disappointed. She stands and turns her back to me.

I'm fine, I think, *except for the fact that now I have two women in my life becoming Jesus freaks.*

Chapter Eighteen

Seth

Father had been in Sychar for a few days before I arrived. My being late because of a mighty hangover normally would not sit well with him. Thankfully he was distracted by his normal illegal activities. I was also thankful Father was not staying with Tabitha and me. I'm not sure who he stayed with. I don't want to know. It would hurt me to know because it would hurt Mother. I try to convince myself it's not what I think, that he's not with someone who gets her water in the heat of the day.

I don't know where Tabitha went or when she will return. She was up and out the door moments after sunrise. The only thing I remember is her leaning down and giving me a gentle kiss on my forehead. She was out and so was I.

I'm hunched over the table with a mug of milk in one hand and a piece of dry bread in the other when the door bursts open. No knock, no greeting, there's just a gruff man still wearing the stench of last night.

"Seth, say your goodbyes to Tabitha tonight," my father says. "We need to get back on the road early in the morning."

"In the morning?" I sit up straight, ready to disagree. "I just got here a few days ago, and I want to spend some more time with Tabitha. I don't get to see her enough as it is. I didn't think we were leaving for Jerusalem for another day or two."

Agitated by my response, Father staggers over to the chair opposite me. He grabs the back and yanks it toward him. He sits down hard. Forming a fist with his left hand he slams it straight down on the tabletop.

"Plans have changed. We're not going to Jerusalem. We're headed to Capernaum. You don't know this, but I have been meeting secretly with some of the high government officials of Caesar's court and some of the high priests. They know we lived in Nazareth and knew Jesus fairly well. Because of our reputation and the traveling nature of our business endeavors, it won't look suspicious for us to be in the same places as Jesus is. It will be merely a convenient coincidence."

I put my mug of milk back on the table. Father's fist is now just a dirty hand pointing at me. I'm not sure I like this idea. But Father goes on. "They want us to learn as much as we can about what he is telling people. They want to know things like what he is doing as he travels from town to town. They don't like Jesus spreading lies like he was sent from a heavenly Father to save our souls."

Father rises from his chair and walks over to the door. He opens it and looks side to side then shuts the door, making sure it is fully closed.

Who does he think is listening?

Satisfied no one is spying on us, he says, "There is growing concern Jesus has recruited others to go out and say that he is some sort of king. He calls them his disciples. Government officials and the high priests are afraid Jesus and his followers are going to cause an uprising; the masses could revolt against the king and his government. And worse, they could revolt against the high priests and their teachings. They don't want things to get out of control because of Jesus' message. One king is enough, and Caesar wants to be it."

I stand up, turn away, and place my hands on my waist. After letting all this sink in during the moment of silence, I turn back around.

"So, you're telling me we've been hired to follow Jesus around like spies and watch his every move. Then we're to report back all we see and hear, right?"

"Yes, that's right. This is an opportunity of a lifetime for us."

Father seems happier than I've seen him in a long time. He walks around the table toward me. For a moment I think this is going to be a special father-son moment. He's going to hug me.

But instead of that special moment, Father reaches behind me grabs the jug of milk, and pours himself a drink.

He's not thinking about me but about gaining wealth and influence. "We're going to make a lot of money and become fast friends with many powerful people in high places. We'll be set for life. We'll want for nothing. It's the easiest thing we've ever done."

He raises the mug and then continues. "The people I met with have stressed that we can't tell anyone what we're doing. We must keep it a secret. You can't tell your mother, or Tabitha, no one."

He lifts the mug to his mouth and tilts his head back. As he drinks, half of the milk spills out over the edge of the mug down his chin and runs into his beard. He slams the empty mug down on the table, causing my half-full mug to fall over. The milk spills onto the dirt floor. Knowing full well what he has just done, a smirk fills his face.

"Tell your woman I'm sorry for the mess I made." He laughs and heads to the door. "I need to go now and get some supplies for our trip tomorrow. Hopefully, your girlfriend will return soon so she can clean up your mess. Don't forget to tell her you're leaving in the morning."

Father leaves. I clean up his mess, pull up a chair, and sit down.

In a matter of seconds, I have gone from being your average, run-of-the-mill criminal, to a secret spy for the king and the high priests of the temples. And I'm not just going to be a spy, but I'm to spy against someone I know, played with as a child, and called a friend.

Can I do this? *Should* I do this? What if Jesus is telling people the truth? I don't want to believe it. Maybe I should.

My head is spinning with all those thoughts, and I wish I had some of that strong wine from the wedding. I look around the room hoping to find something, anything to numb my body, but my search is disrupted when the door opens.

"Honey! I'm home." Tabitha is overly cheerful.

I am not. "Where have you been?" I demand from her as I pound my fist on the table. Rising quickly my chair tumbles backward on the floor. This is out of character for me, a flashback of Father treating Mother like garbage washes over me.

"I've been waiting on you all day."

"All day? It's only just past midday. Sorry about that, but I was following Jesus and the men traveling with him. I wanted to hear more. Plus, I have been sharing my story about the well with whoever is willing to listen. And many are willing. They are now saying they believe what Jesus is telling them."

Feeling bad for my testy response, I give her a hug. "Sorry for sounding like my father. I was just feeling lonely without you. Speaking of Father, he was here." My tone changes as I tell her. "Tabitha, you need to be very careful what you tell people. Some people in high places don't like what Jesus is saying. They're afraid he might start a revolution against the king. Or what if he undermines the high priests and causes many people to follow him? I think he's trying to start some kind of new religion all about him."

She pushes out of our embrace, looking frustrated. "Oh Seth, that is ridiculous. Jesus is not telling people to revolt against the government or start a new religion. With Jesus, it's about having a special relationship with him, not a self-serving religion. He is just telling us about who he is and why he is here. He's not politicking to take over the king's job. Don't you see? Jesus doesn't want people to serve him, but he wants to be a servant to us, to give us something no one else can."

I turn away because I don't want to say anything I will regret, but my mouth opens anyway. "I just don't want you to be taken for a fool. But let's not argue. We only have a short time together. Father and I must leave in the morning."

"In the morning? Why so soon? You just got here."

"I know, but a change in Father's plans demands we leave sooner."

"Can't you go to Jerusalem another time?"

"Part of the change is we are now heading toward Capernaum."

"Capernaum? Jesus and his disciples are heading there. How about I go with you?"

"No!" I say. "You can't go with us. We'll be working, and I'll be too busy to spend time with you. You don't need to hear what he has to say. It's a bunch of lies anyway. Plus, it might get dangerous."

"Dangerous? Why dangerous? What do you mean?"

"Well, I don't know. It just could. I'm telling you, the word on the street is Jesus is making the wrong people mad, very mad. It could get ugly if he doesn't stop preaching his lies. I don't want you in the middle of all that."

Tabitha takes my hands in hers and looks into my eyes. "Seth, you know I love you. I appreciate your concern for me. But you also know I'm a strong, independent woman, capable of making my own decisions. My body does not lessen my brain function. Some might even argue it enhances it." Tabitha adds a chuckle. "So, with love, I say this: I'm going to Capernaum with you or without you."

"You know my father isn't going to like it at all."

"Your Father may tell your mother what she can and cannot do, but I'm not your mother. He'll get over it."

She jumps up and starts to pack her things for the trip.

"Isn't it going to be fun and exciting traveling together! I promise I will travel light." A lilt of victory and joy fills her voice.

How do I tell Father this good news? At least I can tell him I didn't tell her the real reason why we're going to Capernaum.

Chapter Nineteen

Seth

With my eyes barely open, I tilt my head toward a small opening in the side of the house. A dark sky greets me, with no hint of daybreak. The roosters aren't demanding those who are asleep to wake up either.

Father, who is not a bit happy with the news that we now have another traveler, is across the room mumbling something as he checks and rechecks his travel bags. Tabitha sleeps soundly, her eyes closed in peaceful bliss.

I squint my eyes to appear asleep, and I see a fuzzy figure turn toward me with a cup in his hand. Oh no, he'd better not be walking over here to pour water on me. I have experienced that more than my share of times, and it's not pleasant. I raise my head quickly to let Father know I am awake; there's no need for the water torture. To my surprise, he passes me and pours the water over Tabitha's head.

She jumps up and yells, "Old man! What are you doing?"

She is definitely a changed woman. A week ago, she would have called him every nasty name imaginable, plus one or two new ones she made up on the spot. But today she doesn't. Maybe she just wants to kill him.

I rise and move toward Tabitha to stave off the battle of the two hardheaded warriors.

She brushes against my right side, and I grab hold of the hem of her sleep dress, stopping her dead in her tracks.

Father laughs uncontrollably. He bends at the waist and holds the empty cup out in front of him. "I just thought you needed a cup of water. Once you have had my cup of water, you won't want to oversleep ever again!"

Father is mocking her about the *cup of water* Jesus said he had for her. He continues to laugh and then says, "Now get up. It's time to go. If you want to travel with me, you'll learn to stick to a schedule—*my* schedule."

Father grabs his travel bags, throws them over his shoulder, and walks out the door, laughing all the way. Tabitha yanks her left leg forward, which rips the hem of her sleep dress out of my hand. She reaches the door and looks down the path.

"You can't boss me around. I'm not your wife!"

Slamming the door closed, she turns back to me.

"Ugh. Your father makes me so mad. You watch. I'll get him back some way."

"I'm sure you will. But for now, we have to hit the road. We need to be near Capernaum by late afternoon." In minutes, we're out the door following Father.

The walk is long, and the sunlight is ending when we come across a group of people next to the Sea of Galilee. Father says he has no idea why all these people are gathered. A man walks past, and my father stops him to ask, "Sir, are you from around here?"

He says, "Yes, I live in a small village with my family."

"What's going on?" Father asks. "Why are there so many people here?"

"They are here to see the one who calls himself Jesus. This man has been healing the sick, restoring sight to the blind, commanding the lame to get up—they didn't just walk, they ran through the crowds proclaiming Jesus healed them. One had been lame since birth!"

Father pulls me aside and leads me a few steps forward. He looks at me and says under his breath so only I can hear, "See what I'm talking about now? These fools are gathering like dirty, dumb sheep. They're desperate for someone to follow."

I look around to make sure no one is listening.

No one else is close enough to eavesdrop except Tabitha and the man. But they are now talking, so they're both distracted.

Father mumbles on, "Look at all the people gathered here. Jesus is going to cause a revolution if he isn't stopped. Don't forget to write down what this man told us. This is the kind of information they are looking for, and you know who *they* are."

Father then turns and interrupts the conversation between the man and Tabitha. "Sir," he says loudly, "where is this man Jesus now?"

The man points toward a town just south of Capernaum. "He and the men traveling with him got in a boat in Bethsaida and went across the sea in that direction."

That side of the sea has beautiful meadows of lush green grass sprinkled next to the water's edge. It's not heavily populated, but it's a great place to visit if one needs to escape the hectic life in the towns surrounding it.

On most days, the Sea of Galilee has its fair share of fishermen bobbing up and down, looking for the great catch of the day. But today, more boats are sailing than ever before, and they are heading in the same direction as Jesus.

Father tugs on my arm. "Seth, let's hurry and see if we can get a ride on a boat so we can follow Jesus."

Father takes off running toward a row of boats nestled against the shoreline. He waves his hands to get the attention of one of the boat owners who still has room for three good-paying passengers. Tabitha and I grab all the bags and run after him.

Pushing his way through the crowd while knocking over young children and women, Father reaches a fisherman and secures passage on a boat. It's not the most trustworthy-looking boat, but it's a boat, nevertheless. It'd better be good enough to get us there; I don't want to have to swim halfway across this sea.

We board, and the slight wind catches hold of the sail on the mast. Four rowers stagger about on the flat bottom of the boat as the lead fisherman yells orders. The boat bobs and inches closer to the other side of the sea.

The other passengers become excited as we near the area of the beach where the boats are docked. Anxious to get to Jesus, they begin jumping out as soon as they are confident their feet will hit the muddy bottom. The crowd swells larger and larger in a flat open space of meadow.

Tabitha nudges me with her elbow. "Look at all the people here to see Jesus. I want so much to get close enough to see and hear what he says. Do you think it will be possible with all these people here?"

I want to please her, and for selfish reasons, I also want to get close to Jesus. "I'll try my best to get the three of us as close as possible. Maybe we can pay our way to the front."

Once we hit dry land, I get out to help Tabitha disembark and grab our bags. I put the bags under a nearby tree, cover them with leaves, and go back to where Tabitha and Father are waiting.

A narrow path runs up the side of the bank. Everyone else seems to be playing follow-the-leader and joining the crowd forming around Jesus. We take the path that follows the shore, and I see Jesus in the distance, near a large outcropping of rocks. He is reclining against a large rock and talking to several men.

I don't want him to see us coming from behind, so I motion for Father and Tabitha to follow me. We move closer but stay hidden behind the rocks. Tabitha pulls on the back of my tunic. I turn my head back as far as it will go.

"What do you want?" I ask.

"Why are we being so secretive?" she whispers. "Can't we just get closer to him?"

I must think fast to cover up the fact that Father and I are spying. "No..." I am slowly coming up with an idea, "his men would make us go to the back of the crowd. You wanted to get close, didn't you?"

She nods.

"Then be quiet and do as I say."

I'm not sure she wanted me to hear it, but her soft snarky response is "Yeesss, sir."

We're close enough now we can hear what they are saying to one another. That's what I was hoping for. I'm starting to feel like a real spy. Not even Tabitha knows who I am anymore. I'm amazed at how easily I've slipped into a double life.

A voice breaks the silence, and we eavesdrop on Jesus' followers.

"Philip, look out there. Look at all those people. You know it's getting close to dinnertime. All those people have been following us all day, and they're probably hungry."

"I'm kind of getting hungry myself," Philip says.

"Yes, I figured you were. Where are we to buy bread so that these people may eat?"

"Well, the two hundred denarii we have isn't going to be enough to feed a crowd this size."

"I agree. I know what I'm going to do."

I peek over the rocks. One of them walks over to Jesus. He says, "Jesus, there is a small boy who has a burlap sack with five barley loaves and two fish his mother gave him for lunch. He is willing to share, but that won't go far, not with this crowd. Philip could eat that all by himself."

Jesus looks a bit exasperated, like a teacher whose pupil can't add one plus one. He says, "Okay, guys, have the people sit down on the grass in groups of fifty. When you're finished, bring me the boy's lunch."

From behind a bush, Tabitha, Father, and I crouch and watch Jesus' men walk up and down the grassy field organizing people into groups of fifty. Waiting until they are done is going to take a while. I feel my legs tingle, the sure sign that they are slowly falling asleep. So, I wiggle around trying to make myself comfortable.

It's at least an hour before the men return to Jesus. A tall lanky man says, "Jesus, we have all the people sitting in groups of fifty as you asked. Andrew counted the groups of people and stopped counting around five thousand. That doesn't even include most of the women and their children. Here is the sack of food from the boy."

The man hands the sack of five loaves of bread and two fish to Jesus. He lifts the sack high above his head and softly speaks toward the sky as if he is talking to someone in the clouds. I can't make out what he is saying, but he is talking to someone. After a minute, maybe two, Jesus lowers the sack.

He tells his followers, "Take this sack, go to each person, and let them take all the food they want to eat. When they are finished eating and are satisfied, pick up all the pieces that are left over and bring them to me. I don't want any food to go to waste."

Without questioning Jesus, the tall lanky man takes the sack of food, and the other men follow him. They go to each person, in each group. The man opens the sack. One by one they reach in and take out fish and bread, all they desire to eat.

I look over to Father and mouth, "How is the sack of food going to feed five thousand people?"

He looks back and shrugs his shoulders to say, "I have no idea."

As I look over to Tabitha, I notice tears flowing down her cheeks. I lean over and whisper to her, "Why are you crying?"

She nods and softly says, "Can't you see what's going on? Jesus is going to feed all these people out of that little bag of food. That's not possible for you or me to do, but he is doing it. He is providing for others like no other can. He truly is a prophet." Her tears fall faster as she raises both hands to cup her face.

The serving of the meal itself was a miracle. What should have taken all day to pass the fish and bread from one group to the next flowed seamlessly. It was as if time stopped. Afterward, everyone was full, no one needed any more to eat.

Jesus' men go back to each group in a procession. They gather up all the broken pieces of leftover food in baskets. When finished, they take each basket to Jesus and set them on the ground next to him.

I count one, two, three, four . . . twelve baskets sat at Jesus' feet. And each one was filled to the top. Not only did that sack of food feed thousands, but it was also more than enough.

I stare in amazement at all the leftovers, wondering how Jesus was able to perform this trick. Father scoots over to me and says, "His sleight of hand appears to be getting bigger and better, but we'll catch him. We'll expose who he really is soon enough."

After Father makes his proclamation, Jesus tells the tall lanky man to get all the disciples together and take the boat to Capernaum. "I'll join you later," he says.

I turn to Father. "You and Tabitha grab our bags I hid under the tree and head to Capernaum. I'm going to try to follow Jesus and his men. We need to stay as close to them as possible to watch their every move. But we all three can't sneak on their boat together."

Father nods in agreement. Not able to be still long, he moves his legs, which snaps a small branch and sends out a loud cracking sound. The three of us slouch down farther, motionless, holding our breath, hoping we were the only ones to hear it. I look at Father and raise my finger to my lips, shaking my head in frustration.

Seconds pass, and I take a breath and raise my head just enough to peek over the rock. I heave a sigh of relief. Our presence wasn't noticed.

Without moving a muscle or even turning his head my way, Father says, "You're right. We need to stay as close to Jesus and his men as possible. Tabitha and I will meet up with you in Capernaum."

Father then slowly turns his head to Tabitha. "You and I are going to get our bags from under the tree and head to Capernaum. Seth is going to follow Jesus and his men to see if he can hitch a ride on their boat to Capernaum."

"Why can't we go with Seth?" Tabitha sounds suspicious.

I jump in to say, "There won't be enough room on the boat for all three of us."

How much longer can Father and I keep what our real purpose is from Tabitha? She's a smart woman. I know she will begin to catch on sooner or later.

Chapter Twenty

Seth

I catch up to Jesus' men as they near the boat. The sun drops down behind the hills and darkness descends. This makes it easier for me to blend in with the band of brothers.

Just before stepping into the boat, I lift my hood over my head and pull it tight to my face. Only my eyes are exposed. I can tell Jesus' men are tired and not concerned with who is boarding. I scrunch down between the bench seats at the rear of the boat and wrap my hooded robe tightly around my body. I'm just another passenger needing a ride to Capernaum.

No sooner does the boat leave the dock when most, if not all, of the men are fast asleep, snoring in unison. I couldn't have gone to sleep even if I'd wanted to. A nervous excitement fills me as I stow away this close to Jesus' inner circle.

After sailing for about an hour, the boat reaches the deep waters. The gentle winds morph into gales. The boat's soothing sway now turns into erratic bobbing, and water creeps over the sides of the boat. Some of the men jump up from their sleep after cold water splashes them in the face. I continue to crouch in the back of the boat and try to remain unnoticed. The fear of the boat's going under has the men's attention. The fact they have a stowaway on board is the least of their worries.

Suddenly, the tall, lanky man pops up and points toward the back of the boat. "Look!" he shouts.

Oh no, they've discovered their stowaway. I've been made. I mentally prepare to offer an apology and explanation.

But just then the man shouts. "It's a ghost walking on the water!"

Wow! That was a close one.

I lift my head and peer over the back of the bench, trying to see what he is pointing at. The water swishes about at the end of the boat, and I hear other men yell, "It's a ghost! We are going to die!"

Suddenly, a voice speaks from within the waves, "Take courage. It is I. Do not be afraid."

Straining my eyes to see what they are pointing at, I do see what looks like a man's figure walking across the water. I'm not sure what I see, maybe all the bobbing has blurred my vision.

Then another man makes his way close to me when a gust of wind tosses him to the side. Struggling to keep from falling headfirst into the water, he grabs ropes, poles—whatever he can hold on to—to keep from falling overboard. He stays put and yells out to what they are calling a ghost, "Lord, if it is you, command me to come to you on the water."

The response was simply, "Come!"

One of the men in the front of the boat shouts, "Peter! What are you doing? You can't do that! You're going to drown. Stay in the boat!"

Peter doesn't listen. He throws his right leg up and over the side of the boat. Out he goes. I can't believe he's doing this. Now a chorus of men plead for him to get back in. They call him crazy.

I agree with their assessment. I'm not at all confident he will survive this act of foolishness. But it's too late. He can't save himself by grabbing the side of the boat even if he wants to. The winds and waves will toss him right back into the sea.

The voice out in the water says, "Peter, keep your eyes on me. Don't look at the water; just walk toward me. Stay focused."

I don't know if I should jump in to save this crazy man or what. I find myself frozen, unable to move, but I can't take my eyes off Peter. I see him standing on top of the water. The wind swirls like crazy. Peter's hair stands straight out to one side. His tunic flaps in the wind like a sail battling the unseen force of the sea. The noise of the wind is louder than ever, louder than hundreds of chariots racing the great sandstorms of the desert.

And he's *not* sinking. Slowly Peter takes a step, then another, then another. I can't believe what I'm seeing. The winds pick up and the waves grow bigger with every step he takes. Then a scream bounces off the tall waves. "Lord, save me!"

Panic saturates his voice.

"Lord, save me! I'm sinking!"

The water begins to climb up his legs. Then an outstretched hand reaches and takes hold of Peter. "You of little faith, why did you doubt?"

With Peter secure in the man's arms, the two walk to the boat. The winds fade to a gentle breeze and the tall, towering waves lie flat underneath the boat. The quietness of the sea is deafening.

To my surprise, the figure with Peter is Jesus. I quickly turn my face away from him and Peter as the other men help them into the boat.

No sooner does Peter get settled with a blanket wrapped around his shoulders when the "I told you so's" begin.

The tall, lanky one starts by saying, "We told you not to get out of the boat."

Others chime in, "We told you that you would drown."

"We told you—you can't walk on water."

Jesus raises his hand and says, "Stop! Stop telling Peter what he shouldn't have done. Stop judging him. What Peter did was something no one else will ever experience with me again. Yes, Peter took a walk on the water with me. You all sit here spouting off all the reasons why he should not have come to me, but he is the only one here who has cried out to me. Where is your faith, your trust, your cry to me? Is it a matter of convenience or conviction when you cry out to me? What's the boat *you* need to step out of?"

Not another word is spoken the rest of the way to Capernaum. As the boat reaches land, the men gather up their things and busily move about, allowing me the opportunity to sneak off the boat.

As I walk to town to meet up with Father and Tabitha, I have time to figure out what I'm going to tell them. That wasn't just an everyday boat ride. No, I saw not one, but two men walk on water. Tabitha will be so excited. She will believe my story without a doubt. Father will tell me, "They didn't actually walk on top of the water. No, you were closer to the shoreline than you knew, and the water is shallow there, which made it look as if Jesus and Peter were walking on top of the water."

But I know this for sure. We were not close to the shore. You don't have twenty-foot waves near the shoreline. Matter of fact, I saw Peter sinking in the depth of the water, not the shallow area by the shore. Sorry Father, but I saw Jesus and the man named Peter walk on top of the water, not in it. I don't know how to explain it. But I saw what I saw.

Chapter Twenty-One

Seth

I search for Tabitha and Father in Capernaum, all the while fighting exhaustion. I hadn't slept a minute on the boat. The sheer excitement of watching Jesus walk on water astonished me. I couldn't have fallen asleep even if I'd wanted to. Now I want to, but I can't until I find Father and Tabitha.

People are gathered outside the town synagogue. I move closer to find out what's going on. A man is talking to the crowd about Jesus. The listeners quietly stand as the man talks about the many healings and miracles Jesus has done.

I sit on a large rock near the back of the crowd where I can rest for a minute before moving on. I have a story or two I could share if I wanted to, but I don't.

The man finishes one story and goes straight into sharing another. "Listen to the last story I am going to tell you. There was a woman who had been bleeding for twelve years and no one could heal her. She went to doctor after doctor and spent all she had to get well but she only got worse. She heard Jesus was healing many, and she thought, *if only I could touch his cloak, I would get well.*

"Caught in the middle of a massive crowd, she was pushed and shoved around, when suddenly she saw Jesus walking her way. Her only hope to get close was to reach out as far as she could through the multitude of bodies surrounding her. In a desperate attempt, she speared her arm forward and barely touched Jesus' cloak as he passed. Immediately, her bleeding stopped. So did Jesus. He asked the crowd, 'Who is the one who touched Me?'"

"No one said a word, and Jesus spoke again, 'Someone did touch me, for I am aware that power has gone out of me.' The woman, healed by Jesus, went toward him and fell at his feet. Jesus reached down, helped her back up, and said, 'Daughter, your faith has made you well. Go in peace and be healed of your affliction.'"

After the man finishes, the people react in different ways. Part of the onlookers marvel at the story. Others mock him with laughter and shout, "Jesus, come heal me! Let me touch your magical cloak!"

The man walks away, and most of the people follow close behind him, asking for more stories.

As people separate, a woman remains. She's on her knees with her head buried in her hands. After taking a longer look, I think the woman might be Tabitha. I shake the fatigue away, force myself up off the rock, and walk toward her.

She reaches her arms up to the sky and tilts her head back toward the clouds. She cries out, "Jesus, Lord, I desire faith like the woman who needed only to believe that if she just touched the hem of your cloak, she would be healed. I seek from you the boldness to tell others you are truly the great physician, healer of our bodies and our souls. The faith I hold I pray will conquer my fears of life's failures of yesterday . . . today . . . tomorrow."

"Tabitha?"

Startled, she lowers her arms to her chest. Her expression switches from prayerful to playful in an instant. "There you are! Your father and I didn't know how we were going to find one another." She wipes tears from her eyes nonchalantly as if she hadn't just been crying out to God. "Just a minor detail we forgot to nail down last night."

We both chuckle.

I offer her a hand. She takes it and pulls herself off the ground.

"Yeah," I say. "We should have figured out how the meetup was going to happen. No big deal now. I found you. Where is Father?"

"I'm not sure. All he said was that he had to meet with some people, and he would be back by dinnertime. Who do you think your father is meeting? Does this have anything to do with us following Jesus?"

"Who knows? You know my father. He goes one direction and then ten others." I hope that answer will satisfy her and she will drop the questions. To change the subject, I say, "Last night was amazing."

"Why? What happened to you last night? Were you able to hitch a ride on the boat with Jesus and his men?"

"Tabitha, let's find a place to sit down. I have a lot to tell you, and I'm too tired to stand here and tell you."

She leads me to a room Father rented. It's tiny, with a small table resting against the back wall. Why had he rented such a small place? He can afford a bigger, better place. He is so tight with his money. His middle name should be Frugal.

Three wooden chairs surround the table. One lamp, a pot, and three cups hang on a piece of iron stretching across the back wall. A community fire pit was out back for cooking purposes. There's barely enough room for three sleep mats on the floor.

I don't mention the damp feel of the room or the worn rug. "Not the king's palace, but it will work. We probably won't be staying more than a day anyway. Jesus doesn't stay too long anywhere in his travels these days."

Tabitha nods. "The room will be fine. All we need is a place to sleep. I'll start a fire and heat some warm water."

"A warm drink sounds great. It got chilly on the lake last night, and I'm still trying to get warm."

The warm mug, cupped in both my hands, hits the spot. It's giving me a renewed energy. I'm ready to talk now. "Okay, Tabitha, grab a chair and come sit next to me. Let me tell you what happened last night."

She slides a chair and positions it on my right side. "What happened? It has to do with Jesus, right?"

I take a breath and begin. "I got on the boat without anyone seeing me or saying a word. I covered my head and slipped down between two wooden benches in the back of the boat. Within minutes of leaving the shore, the men fell fast asleep. We sailed for an hour, and then the winds picked up and the boat rocked hard side to side."

"Oh, no! Were you scared?"

"Not yet. But the tall skinny man we saw with Jesus jumps up and yells, 'It is a ghost, walking on the water!'"

"A ghost? There was a ghost out in the lake?"

"No, Tabitha, it wasn't a ghost. It was Jesus. And he wasn't *in* the water. He was walking *on* the water."

"On the water? What do you mean? Were you next to the shore? Were there big rocks under the water?"

"No, we were out about three or four miles from the shoreline, in the middle of the lake where there are no rocks to walk across. Then this guy named Peter yells back to Jesus, 'Lord if it is you, command me to come to you on the water.' Jesus tells him to come. Now all the other men are screaming at Peter and telling him to stay in the boat. They are blasting him with ridicule and calling him crazy."

"Wow! Are you kidding me? Did this truly happen?" Tabitha scoots her chair closer to mine and leans in, as if not to miss a word.

"No, I'm not kidding. This guy Peter walked on the water!"

All excited, Tabitha clasps her hands at her chin.

"Seth, don't you see what is happening? Jesus is trying to teach us and show us what faith in him is all about. It is not about what we can do on our own. It's about what he wants to do for us. He wants us to believe in him, trust him, keep our eyes on him, and stay focused on him. It's like the sick woman did—she reached out in faith."

It's interesting to me that Tabitha mentions the healing of the woman even though she doesn't know I heard the man tell the story. But she has a point. A lot of what I'm seeing does revolve around the theme of faith in Jesus.

"Yes, Tabitha, I see a theme here with Jesus."

I look down at the dirt floor and rub my hand through my hair, trying to find the right words to say next. "I have seen and heard enough to make me question my life. I don't know what I believe. I feel so confused."

"Confused? Seth, what do you mean?"

"I'm confused that most times my head tells me it's okay to steal, rob, lie, and do the things I do. Then sometimes my heart or something deeper tells me there's more to life. I should seek a different path."

"Please don't run from the voice that tells you there is more to life than this. I believe we have a greater purpose. We just don't know what that is yet. We can make a difference if we trust Jesus and ask him to show us the way. We can focus on him, reach out to him even when we can't see him."

"Tabitha, I hope what you say is true for you. But it's not for someone like me. I have done some terrible things. You know me. I have taken from people, I have hurt people, some beyond hurt—they're not coming back. You know I have never uttered an honest prayer. I've gone into a temple for worship, but I've gone to take money out of the offering box, but never put anything in. I'm one of those people who is not worthy, not good enough. It's too late for someone like me to ever be forgiven or to merit a place in God's heaven."

Agitated, I stand up and look away from her. "Plus, I like what I do. I like the things that come from stealing from others. But you? You still have a chance. If that is what you want, then I say go for it. I will miss you and always love you, but it's too late for me. My fate has been set."

She must have stood too because I felt her hand on my shoulder. She turns me back toward her.

"Oh, Seth, stop saying that. I don't believe your fate has been set. You're still breathing, aren't you? You also know me. Have I lived a perfect life? Doing what's right all the time? Not even close. Let's not list all my past husbands and boyfriends. I am such an outcast at home that I have to go to the well when no one else will be there to shame me further with their stares. I may not have done some of the things you have, but you haven't done some things I have. I don't think there is a sin scale. Sin is sin. Welcome to the club."

"I believe God sent Jesus here specifically for people like us, so we can be free from our sins. But we must believe and trust in him and change the way we live our lives. We need to seek his way of living. We'll never be perfect at it, but I believe he will be there to reach out and pull us from the deep waters of life's struggles, just as he did for Peter. I believe Jesus wants us to walk to him, believing and trusting as Peter did. That's the good news he is trying to tell us."

The room falls silent. I grab the chair and sit back down. I tilt backward and stare at the ceiling.

Then the door breaks open, and Father stumbles in. His pungent breath adds evidence he has had too much strong drink.

"Seth!" Father slurs. "Well, you made it. I wasn't sure you would find us. You aren't the brightest navigator when you need to get somewhere. I was afraid it might take days to find you. Once or twice I even thought maybe I would be better off without having you around, slowing me down. But too bad, you're here now."

Who needs a whip to rip through you when words can tear you apart, causing even deeper wounds?

Tabitha looks at me with tears sliding down her cheek. She whispers, "Seth, he's drunk. He didn't mean it."

I see her beautiful tear-filled face. Wanting to believe

her, I say, "It doesn't matter if he does or doesn't. He's my father."

Chapter Twenty-Two

Seth

I hate waking up groggy, feeling as if I haven't slept a wink. I'm still replaying in my head the conversation Tabitha and I had last night. And of course, I'm mulling over the last words of the night, beautifully spoken by a drunken man, who was slurring and spitting out heartfelt words, telling his son he would be "better off" without him around. If that doesn't give cause for a restless night, I don't know what will.

Father comes to life on his sleep mat in the exact same position he fell onto it. Rubbing his head and moaning, he rolls over on his stomach and slowly rises to his knees. He reaches out and grabs the small table. It leans over almost to the point of no return. The cups drop to the floor. He picks up a cup and hurls it my way. His aim is off about two feet to the left. The cup rolls to a stop just inches from Tabitha's head.

"Seth, get up," Father says. "Go follow Jesus."

That's interesting. Tabitha tells me I should follow Jesus, now Father. I chuckle to myself and think, *not for the same reason.*

Talking loud enough to wake up the whole block, Father says, "Did you hear me, boy? You need to follow Jesus to see what he is going to do today."

Tabitha is now showing life as well. She rubs the sleep

from her eyes and looks across the tiny room. She is close enough I could reach out and touch her.

She says, "Seth, don't leave without me. I want to go with you."

"Father," I ask, "are you going, too?"

"No, I have to do something else," he snarls.

"Care to share what?" I pick up the cup, which miraculously, didn't break.

"I can't. Your girlfriend is here. She doesn't need to know what we're doing. Don't you remember? We are to keep it to ourselves. I told you she shouldn't have come with us. She needs to go."

His face turns pale. I fear he's about to hurl. This time from his mouth. It wouldn't be the first time he got sick from too many drinks.

But Father keeps his drinks down and runs out the door, slamming it shut behind him.

"Your Father knew I was right here, right? I heard every word he said."

"Sure, that's his loving way of telling you to get lost. You're not wanted. It doesn't matter if he meant to hurt you or not, that's my father. Welcome to the family."

Having forced my way off the mat, I wash my face and down two cups of milk. "Tabitha, it's time to go."

I step outside into the bright, warm morning sun when Tabitha tugs on my robe from behind. This stops me in my tracks, and she turns me halfway around. "What did your father mean when he said I didn't need to know what you were doing? That you're to keep it a secret? What's the secret?"

I glance down, not sure how to respond so I decide to make something up. This way we appear to be the good guys, not the bad guys. "Well, Father and I have been hired to follow Jesus and his men to make sure nothing bad happens to them."

I'm not sure she buys that, but she does ask, "Nothing

bad happens? What does that mean? Who hired you?"

"I can't tell you yet," I answer. "I will one day. I just can't right now. They are afraid some people might want to hurt Jesus and his men for what they are preaching. You know, not everyone likes what Jesus is doing."

With a look of contempt, she looks my way. "Yes, and your father is one of them. Why would he care about Jesus' safety? That doesn't make sense to me."

I realize I did not satisfy her curiosity. I may have made it worse.

"Trust me, it is all good. I will be able to tell you more soon. But you can't let Father know you know this much. He would kill us both if he thinks you know anything. Please tell me you won't say a word about this to him."

With a worried tone, she whispers, "I won't. He wouldn't really kill us. That's just a matter of speech, right?"

"Right," I whisper. In my head I think, *yes, he probably would kill us. He is a man with no forgiveness or grace in his cold stone heart. I know that from what I have seen him do to others.*

"Tabitha, come on. Let's go. It's getting late. We need to go see what Jesus is up to. It's a good thing we are doing, trust me."

She follows, but I don't think she is convinced of what I said. I'm not either.

I hate that I lied to her.

That's going to come back to me in a bad way. I know it will. She will hate me for sure when she learns the real reason we are following Jesus. She won't forgive me either. Will anyone ever find reason to forgive me? Probably not. I don't deserve it.

Tabitha and I walk down several streets looking for Jesus and asking passersby if they know where he is. We turn a corner and see a large group of people gathered around a two-story house in a row of similar houses.

We look at each other and know we must have found

him. Without saying a word, we run in that direction. The front door is packed with people trying to get in. A small walkway makes a path between the houses. I head to the back of the building and motion for Tabitha to follow me. To our sad surprise, just as many people are trying to get in the back door. I'm about to give up when I hear Tabitha whisper-scream my name. I turn around, and she is pointing to the ground, waving frantically for me to come back to her.

"Look, Seth, it's a small opening underneath the house."

Some of the bigger homes had underground pits for storage. The pits helped keep wine cool.

"If we move this piece of wood that's covering the opening, we might be able to crawl through and see what's going on."

Before I can even offer my opinion, Tabitha is on her knees scooting her way through. I kneel and size up the width and height of the opening. I'm not sure my big rear end will fit. I crawl forward, trying to keep up with Tabitha. It's very dark except when the shimmer of candlelight drops between the floor cracks. All of a sudden, my forward crawl comes to an abrupt halt. My head meets the heel of Tabitha's sandal.

"Seth, can you scoot over a little closer to me?" she whispers her directions.

I scoot closer, and we can now sit up. Right in front of us is a square decorative wall covering. We can see through the slits into the room, which is filled to capacity. It is dark enough in the pit that we are sure that they can't see us. The angle of the pit doesn't allow us to see any higher than a foot or two off the floor. That limits our range of vision to seeing only legs and feet.

Tabitha puts her finger to her lips reminding me to be quiet. The people in the crowded room find their places. An empty chair sits in the middle of the room. Then I see the legs of a man stop in front of a chair. He sits down.

A hush covers the room.

"Ask! Ask me what you want to ask." It's Jesus' voice.

Another voice off to the side of the room speaks up. "Jesus, you say you are the light of the world. And whoever follows you will never walk in darkness but will have the light of life. You are saying this as your own witness, on your own behalf. We need more proof."

"Okay, so you need more than my word. I know where I came from, where I'm going—but you don't. You think you know what you know, you judge by your understanding. I'm not judging anyone. I am who I say I am, and the father who sent me knows exactly who I am."

"Okay, Jesus, so who is your Father? Where is he? We haven't seen him."

Jesus moves his legs to the right. I can't see what he is doing with his upper body.

"Oh, but you are wrong. You have seen me, so you have seen my father. If you truly knew me, you would also know my father."

The room erupts in voices of dissent and voices of acceptance. Then pieces of ceiling beam hit the floor, stirring up dust all around Jesus' feet. He turns back around.

The room becomes quiet to a deafening silence.

"Please lower him." It's Jesus speaking again.

I'm not able to see what is happening, so I lean over to Tabitha and ask, "What's going on? Can you see what's going on?"

She shakes her head. "Hold on," she whispers.

After about five minutes dust is still slipping down from above.

"A mat with a rope tied to all four corners has lowered," Tabitha says. "A man is lying on it."

Once this man is resting safely on the floor, Jesus says, "Son, get up off your mat. I forgive your sins. Your friends have made a tremendous effort to bring you to me by lowering you through the ceiling. They have great faith. Get up, your legs are no longer dead. Pick up your mat and go back home."

The man jumps up off his mat. Tabitha reaches back and grabs my hand. With her other hand, she covers her mouth in amazement.

Voices throughout the room say things like, "Jesus can't say that."

"That's blasphemy!"

"Only God can forgive someone's sins."

Then Jesus speaks up, "Why do you say I can't? I am the son of God, having authority to forgive sins." He stands and walks away from the chair.

Some in the room shout and praise what they witnessed, making their declaration of belief in Jesus known.

The room begins to clear out. So, I reason Jesus must have left. Tabitha and I don't move. Maybe it's because our muscles are numb from sitting in the same position for too long. Or we are numb from what we have witnessed.

The room is empty now except for the chair and two sets of men's legs. The men must have thought they were alone because one of them says, "The only way to shut Jesus up is to kill him."

I tug on Tabitha's robe and lean my head to one side, indicating it's time to go.

Chapter Twenty-Three

Aran

I stop pacing back and forth in the room that is now almost empty. Minutes ago it was filled wall-to-wall with people listening to Jesus. And they supposedly witnessed another miracle. But it was obviously a trick. The man was an actor, paid to pretend to be healed.

Jesus is gone. The fools who helped him with his little "healing" are gone. There's just a handful of people debating who's right and who's wrong huddled across the room.

I stop pacing and make my point again to my companion. "Saul, listen to me, you know the only way we're going to shut Jesus up is to kill him. You've 'shut up' others who were proclaiming teachings contrary to what the high officials wanted spoken."

I look around the room, making sure my conversation stays between the two of us. "I've seen you go into house after house carrying people off to prison, beating them to near death, and even silencing some permanently when necessary. So why is Jesus any different?"

Saul whirls around. His finger points aggressively at my face. "Slow down a minute," he says. "Don't get too far out in front of this thing. Not all the high priests want it handled that way." His finger gets closer to my face with every word. I step back until the wall forces me to stop. I'm just a word or two from having a finger in my eye. His eyes glare, refusing to give in. He adds to his argument. "And some of the high officials think throwing him in a dark hole, hiding him away for a long time will change his mind, that he would eventually stop telling people he is the Son of God. It might go away quietly." With both hands Saul gestures, emphasizing his last words.

"Aran, this is different. Jesus has stirred up a lot of people in a way that I've never seen before. His charisma makes him popular and therefore dangerous. We have to be careful not to cause a mass revolt of the people."

Saul steps back to give me some distance, folding his arms in front of him.

Feeling his wrath has abated, I gently throw out these words: "The longer Jesus can tell people his lies and have actors help him perform fake miracles, the more cleanup you and the high officials will have to do. I say let's stop him sooner than later."

This time Saul raises his hand, palm open. I squint thinking, *I really made him mad this time*, waiting for a slap to fall across my face. I see the blurry figure step back from me. He puts his hand under his chin as if he is seriously contemplating what I said.

"You have to admit the so-called 'miracles' are pretty amazing. It's hard to explain how Jesus is doing them, even if he is getting help from people."

Confident we are back to being partners again, I open my eyes wide. "Tell me you aren't falling for his trickery. Man, wipe away the scales of fantasy from your eyes so you can see who Jesus actually is. Walk with your eyes wide open so you aren't blinded by his deception."

Saul reaches out with both hands and takes hold of my arms below my shoulders. "Yes, you're right. I will never be blinded by his preaching or his healing tricks. If you pay enough, people will do anything for you. I will fake an illness for the right amount of money. I know, Aran, you have a price."

After a good laugh, Saul looks at me. Without any doubt in his voice, he says, "Never will you hear me say a good word about Jesus. He should be stopped and stopped for good. Jesus will be heading back to Jerusalem for the Passover in the next day or two. Word has it one of his closest followers is willing to help us trap him so we can arrest him in Jerusalem. His name is Judas. Like you, he is willing to do anything for a few silver coins."

Saul gave me half a grin. That odd smile coupled with his mocking tone made me unsure if his statement was a compliment or a thinly veiled insult. I shrugged. Doesn't matter, he's right. Throw a few coins my way, and I would hand over my own son.

Saul got back to business. "I need you and Seth ready to head back to Jerusalem when Jesus does. Don't let him out of your sight. Your reports will be helpful when the high priests put together a plot for Jesus' arrest. Now go and get ready. Time is coming soon for Jesus to be stopped."

He places his hands on top of my shoulders, and with his face just inches from mine, he chuckles when he says, "Aren't you excited to be part of Jesus' last days? Who knows, you might be forever known as the guy who exposed Jesus for who he is."

Saul takes his hands off my shoulders and adjusts the tunic around my neck. "Don't forget, Seth will also be right up there with you."

Saul steps back, turns, and walks out of the room.

During the entire walk to the rented room, I think about the role I'm playing in what is going to happen to Jesus and, of course, to Seth. Trapping Jesus will set us apart from all others. If only my father could see me now. Maybe, just maybe, he would be proud of me.

I reach the room and open the door to find Seth and Tabitha sitting at the table having a cup of milk and sharing a loaf of bread.

"Hate to interrupt your cozy dinner, but, Seth, what have

you been up to today? "

I grab a chair, turn it backward, and sit down uncomfortably close to the lovely couple.

"A nice picnic with your girlfriend? I haven't seen you all day. I thought I told you to follow Jesus. All you had to do was follow Jesus. You can't even do something that simple."

Without asking, I reach for the last bit of bread and stuff it in my mouth.

"Father, we did."

"I didn't see you there," I say as I spray pieces of bread all over the table. I don't care about the mess.

"No, you didn't, that's how good we are at being hidden, not seen. I'm starting to get good at this spy stuff. Tabitha is pretty good, too."

Ignoring the mess I made, Seth moves his chair so I can see his excitement about what he wants to tell me.

"We? Please don't tell me your girlfriend was with you."

Without looking her way, I sense her desire to enlighten me.

"I have a name. It's Tabitha. And yes, I was there, too."

Out of the corner of my eye, I see her straighten up in her chair.

"If it wasn't for me, we wouldn't have been able to see and hear what went on in the big house where Jesus was speaking. You're welcome."

Tabitha goes on. "It's a good thing we were there, too."

Growing impatient, I interrupt her. "Settle down. I'm sure whatever you witnessed wasn't that big of a deal."

"Well, if you would be quiet for a moment, I will tell you what we heard."

She pauses, waiting for my rapt attention, I suppose. I smile at her as I would a spoiled toddler.

She continues. "We heard two men talking after Jesus left, discussing having to stop him from continuing his teachings by killing him!"

That got my attention, rapt and instant.

"Where were you?" I ask, perhaps with too much interest. "I was there, and I didn't see either one of you in the house."

Seth joins in. "That's because we weren't in the room, we were underneath it."

He makes motions with his arms as if he's crawling. "We couldn't get in," Seth says, now pointing to his girlfriend, "but Tabitha found a small opening on the side of the house, and we crawled in. We were able to watch what was going on up to three feet off the floor. And we could hear everything."

I have to think fast here since I'm sure Tabitha will circle back to the *killing Jesus* conversation. We need her to think our job is to help protect Jesus, not that we're the ones helping to stop Jesus dead in his tracks.

"Tabitha," I say, trying to sound genuine while forcing a smile, "that's great information. You learned about someone who wants to kill Jesus. That's what Seth and I are here for—to try and gather information like that to help guard against anything bad happening to him. Good job."

I reach out to take her hands in mine and she recoils faster than a snake.

Glancing over to Seth, my expression tells him, "Don't say a word." Out loud I say, "Did you and Seth see who the two men were?"

Tabitha's fingers are tightly entangled with each other and resting high on her lap. "No, just the sandals of one guy and his legs up to his knees. He was standing in front of the wall covering we could see through. We could hear the second man pacing back and forth on the far side of the open room, so we couldn't see his feet as well. He was the one proposing to kill Jesus."

To confirm she doesn't know whom the voice belonged to, I ask, "What did he sound like? Could you recognize the voice if you heard it again?"

She drops her head, looking dejected. "No, I don't think

so," she answers. "He spoke just loud enough for me to hear what he was saying but softly enough I couldn't make out any kind of special inflections in his voice."

"Oh, that's too bad," I say, relieved. I slap my hands on my knees. "Well, it's been a big day. We should go to sleep." I jump up. "We need to be rested for our trip back to Jerusalem. Jesus will be heading that way in the next day or two. We have to follow him even closer now. We need to make sure he gets back to Jerusalem safe and sound."

Seth leans across the small table and gives Tabitha a peck on her cheek. Then he takes his place on his bed mat against the wall to my left. Tabitha walks over to her bed mat, which is stretched out against the opposite wall and lying left to right at our feet. Being the last to take my place on the floor, I slip off my sandals and set them off to my side. It feels good to be in bed. It's been a long day.

I drift in and out of sleep, and I hear a noise that wakes me completely. I open my eyes just enough for me to peek out unnoticed. Tabitha has one of my sandals in her hand, holding it up close to her eyes. She turns it around and looks at one side, then with a quick spin to the sandal, she inspects the heel. After a minute or two passes, she sets the sandal back down, making sure it is in the exact same place I left it.

Then she lies down and flips over, facing the wall. The silence of the night is broken by the sound of her crying. My eyes start to fill with water, and I'm not sure why. Dismissing it, I wipe my eyes dry and drift back to sleep.

Chapter Twenty-Four

Seth

Father is out of the house already. I bend over to tie my sandals when I catch the scent of his leather strap that he carries as if it were still lying on the floor next to me. It's the same smell his whip had when he waved it in my face, trying his best to intimidate his young boy to be the perfect son he hoped for.

I rub my eyes, stretch my arms to the ceiling, and see Tabitha sitting at the table cuddling a cup, steam rising out the top with a strong hint of mint not far behind. It smells great. It takes me back to when Mother would have a warm drink on cold mornings waiting for me to get up and share a cup with her before we started our day. It's amazing how smells can take you back to a time when it was either a time you cherished or a time you wished to forget.

"Good morning," I say. "That smells great."

"It is. Come. I will pour you a cup."

She hands me the cup, which is almost too hot to hold. I take a sip, burning the tip of my tongue. "Wow, that's hot."

"Sorry about that. I did say it was hot. Sit it down before you spill it all over yourself."

I set the cup down, shake the burning sensation from my hand, and grab the chair with my other hand. Sitting next to her I carefully pick up the mug so I don't spill.

"I wonder why your father left so early. I woke up way

before daybreak, and he was already gone."

I avoid direct eye contact. "Who knows, maybe he went to get more supplies for our return trip to Jerusalem."

She tilts her head and seems unconvinced. "That early?" she asks. "I doubt it. Are you sure you know what your father is doing and what he has got you involved with?"

Willing to burn my lips, I take a big sip, trying to think of the right response.

"I told you Tabitha, we were hired to follow Jesus and look out for him. I'm sure Father is just checking to make sure everything is all right. It's a big responsibility, you know."

I thump the cup down on the table spilling hot water on my hand. It takes a lot for me not to blurt out a foul word or two. I'm doubly agitated by her drilling me about Father, and I shout, "Why are you so concerned with what Father is doing?"

Able to go toe to toe with any man, she slaps her hands down on her hips and shouts back, "Seth, remember those two men standing in front of the wall covering talking about killing Jesus?"

"Yes, dear, I do." I lower my tone.

"Well, I remembered seeing something on one of the man's sandals. It was a black scuff mark." She removes her hands from her hips. After successfully bringing me back down to a civil tone she continues. "But this is what stands out about that scuff mark, it looked like a fish. The shape reminded me of a tiny fish. That's why I remember the scuff mark."

"A fish?" I ask in disbelief.

"Yes, I know that sounds weird, but it reminded me of a tiny fish."

With great sarcasm and exaggerated body movements I reply, "Okay, we'll start our search first thing today. We'll get down on our hands and knees and look at every sandal in town to see if we can spot the killer fish. I mean the killer wearing a fish."

I chuckle waiting for Tabitha to follow. It doesn't happen.

"Seth, you idiot! I think I know who the man is."

"Look case solved already. Please tell me who the mystery man is so we can call the guards and have this man brought to justice."

I am shamelessly trying to bring some lightness to the conversation because it is getting harder and harder for me to not just blurt out what the truth is.

She takes hold of my face with her right hand under my chin and turns it in her direction. "Seth, I think the man is your father."

Snapping my face out of her gentle grasp and turning away, I yell, "Father! No way. Why do you think it's him?"

"Last night, after you and your father fell asleep, I looked over and saw his sandals on the floor next to him. Something caught my eye, so I picked one up, and that's when I remembered seeing the scuff mark on the sandal of the man standing in front of us. The same scuff mark is on your father's sandal."

I jump up, causing my chair to fall backward to the ground. "Tabitha, that's crazy. Sandals worn long enough will have scuff marks on them. What looks like a fish to one person might look like a dog to someone else. I think you are just tired and starting to see things that aren't real."

She raises a finger to show she has an idea. "I can prove to you your father was one of two men talking about killing Jesus. Not only does the scuff mark match, but I can tell the color and thickness of your father's sandals are identical to the man standing in front of us. The man saying Jesus must be killed."

I bend down and forcefully pull off one of my sandals. Holding it out in front of her face, I reply, "Look at all the scuff marks on my shoes. Oh, look I see a sheep. No, it's a pig. See how it can look like anything you want it to be."

Agitated, I throw the sandal behind me. "Tabitha, my father would never want to hurt Jesus."

I compose myself and take hold of her arms. Pulling her closer to me, I take my right hand and gently brush her hair from her eyes. "Maybe it would be best if you go back home and let Father and me finish our job by ourselves. Father was right, you shouldn't have come with us. I will give you what you need for the trip and hire a caravan to take you back home. We can meet up again after the job is over."

She pushes away from me. Raising both hands she pulls her hair away from her face and looks straight at me. "Seth, I don't need anything from you. I'm a big girl. I was taking care of myself long before you came along. You keep your money. It's more important to you than I am anyway."

Father walks in and sees the intense conversation we are having. He laughs and says, "What's wrong? Are you all fighting over who's going to do the dishes?"

Tabitha heads toward him.

I think, *oh no! She's going to slap him*, when she suddenly falls in front of him and grabs his sandals.

Trying to keep his balance, Father shouts, "Crazy woman, what are you doing? Take your hands off my sandals."

She stops and looks up at Father. "These aren't your sandals. At least they aren't the sandals you had last night."

"Yes, you are correct," he says. "I thought I would treat myself, so I bought a new pair. Do you like them?" Father moves his feet back and forth as if he is modeling the latest fashion.

Tabitha gets up on her feet and walks out the door. I start after her when Father grabs me by my arm, squeezing with force. He looks me right into my eyes with a dark expression I haven't seen in a while.

"Let her go," he says. "Get your stuff ready. We are leaving today—without her. She is starting to be a problem we don't need. I would hate for her to stay with us and something bad happen to her, wouldn't you?"

With that said Father releases my arm. I don't want harm to come to Tabitha. I must do what Father demands. The thought of something bad happening to her makes my heart pound. Like it might burst inside me. My heart aches at the thought of never seeing her again.

Chapter Twenty-Five

Mary

After sitting for hours at the loom, I look down and frown at my red puffy fingers. Handling the wool, turning it into thread, and then constantly moving it through the loom take a toll on my hands. As each movement becomes monotonous, my mind wanders to years past when Joseph would walk through the front door for a bite of lunch. Although our ages were separated by quite a few years, there was a special connection between us. Jesus was the number one special connection we shared.

I miss Joseph. He has been gone far too long. But I promised him I would raise our son to be the one God wanted him to be. I think I have done that. I hope so. Missing Joseph makes me miss Jesus, too. He loved Joseph. It was a tremendous loss for Jesus when Joseph died. He grew up continuing to learn the trade his father taught him.

One day when Jesus was about nine years old, he ran into the house carrying a chair and shouted, "Look, Mother, what I just made!" He proudly set it down by the meal table and jumped onto the seat. As he moved, the chair moved. The legs were not all equal lengths. They were off just enough to make the chair wobble side to side as he shifted with excitement.

"Mother, this is the first chair I have ever made. Father

said it was perfect for that special person."

Joseph was so proud of Jesus. He was proud of all his children, but Jesus was special, like the chair he made.

As Joseph got older, his lunch visits would get longer and longer as he wanted to rest his back or just take a quick nap. I could see my dear husband grow a little weaker each day.

I would gently shake his shoulder and whisper, "Joseph, you'd better get going. You know I love having you come home for lunch, but you need to get back to the workshop."

As he staggered to his feet, fighting the stiffness of joint pain, he would whisper, "Yes, dear."

I'd follow him to the door with one hand gently holding his arm to make sure his legs were awake enough to carry him.

"Mary, I'm okay," he would say. "Stop treating me like the old man I am. Age is just a number. Please forget my number is more than twice yours, will you?"

We both would laugh. As he passed through the door, he would faithfully touch the mezuzah on the doorpost with his finger and then put his finger to his mouth and blow a kiss to me. I always returned his kiss with one of my own.

I still love him just as much today as I did when I learned our life would change dramatically with the miracle birth—the gift of Jesus.

Knock! Knock! The loud thumps snap me out of my daydreams. I jump up, nearly tripping over the wool gathered at my feet.

"I will be right there." I open the door, and my heart tumbles with joy. "Jesus! Is it really you?" I leap toward my son and give him the biggest hug yet. He smells of the sea and sweat and olive oil.

"Yes, Mother. I am truly here!" His smile crooks upward. "My friends and I are on our way to Jerusalem, and I thought I would stop for a little while to say hello. I can't stay long. I hope you don't mind."

"Mind? Why would I mind? But I do wish you were here more. I miss you so much."

With my arm hooked into his, I walk him into the house over to the kitchen table. I begin rattling off the jumble of thoughts in my head: "Here, sit down. Rest. Let me get you a cup of cold water. How about something to eat? You must be hungry. I have leftover fish and some bread. Everything is still warm."

Jesus doesn't sit at the table. "Mother, slow down. You are speaking faster than I can listen. Please, take a breath. I know you are excited to see me. I am glad to see you, too. Yes, it's been too long I know, but I had to go away. My time has come. I want to share some things with you that are going to happen to me. I want you to hear it first."

I turn and look him directly in the eyes. "What do you mean?" I ask. "You're scaring me. I don't want anything bad to happen to you."

"Mother, I will say to you what I have said to my disciples: 'I am the way, and the truth, and the life; no one comes to the Father but through me.' Because of the things I have said, the healings and miracles I have performed, many want to silence me."

"Silence you? What do you mean?"

"Mother, they don't want me proclaiming the good news. I offer a gift for all the people, for every generation, today, and generations to come. I bring the good news that God loves them and wants to forgive their sins. God wants all to receive His grace. For God so loved the world, he gave his Son—me—that whoever believes in me, shall not perish, but have eternal life. For the truth to be fulfilled, I must suffer greatly, be put to death, and finally, I will be raised on the third day."

"Jesus, are you saying that someone will kill you? No! No! Please tell me that's not what you're saying. Who would want you dead just because they don't like what you're saying?"

I turn my back to my son. I can tell my face is turning red with anger. I don't want him to see the rage in me. No mother wants to bury her child.

He hugs me from behind and speaks softly in my ear. "Mother, you and all who have read the Scriptures from generation to generation know what they say. Yes, many still don't fully understand, but I am the one who has been sent to atone, to carry the sins of all from now to forever. I am the Good News."

I shake my head. Every nerve in my body is on fire.

"Everyone is a sinner, Mother. But I am here to save them. Everyone has sinned. No matter who they are or who they think they are, all are sinners, every last one. And the hard truth is the payment for sin is death. It's that simple."

"Then let *them* die," I whisper. "Not you."

"God has provided a way to pay that sin debt—me. I am the way to everlasting life. I am to pay the debt, their debt. I will put the sins of everyone on my back and carry them away. I am beyond enough for all."

I look for a loophole in his logic. "But there are many good people," I say. "Those who work hard at the synagogue, for example. Those who offer acceptable sacrifices."

I glance over my shoulder. His expression is mellow with sadness. I can tell he's disappointed I don't understand, that I don't embrace his death plan, and hate those who will take part in it.

He sighs and says, "No one can do enough, be good enough to deserve eternal life in God's heavenly paradise. No, they can't do enough and no, they don't have to do enough to receive salvation. God's grace is free to all who say yes and believe that I am. There is no list of to-dos. No mark to hit to be rewarded with eternal life in heaven. For by grace, you will be saved through faith. It is the gift of God, not of works. Until the last breath you breathe, anyone can call on me, for God's Grace."

I turn around and this time look deeply into my son's eyes. Seeing his sincerity, I feel ashamed. Ashamed of how I responded. The rage and hate within me for the idea and the people who would carry it out.

"Jesus, please forgive me for the rage and hate I have for those who want to hurt you. I believe what you have shared is the truth, but is there any other way that it can be done so you don't have to suffer, to die? Can you tell someone who can protect you? Perhaps the temple guards or the high priests? Don't stop there. Go straight to the top, the governor, Pilate. Maybe he can help you."

Jesus slowly looks down at me and says softly, "Mother, like them you can be forgiven because you too don't know what you are doing. Please don't forget what I said will happen. I will be raised on the third day. They may beat me, kill me, put my body in a tomb, but they will not be able to silence me. I will be resurrected. You will see me again in my full glory. You'll just have to wait three days."

I lean forward and take Jesus in my arms. My mind immediately floods with the memory, going back more than thirty years ago, when the angel Gabriel came to me and said, "Mary, do not be afraid, for you have found favor with God. You will conceive in your womb and bear a son, Jesus. He will be great and will be called the Son of the Most High."

As I am reminded of that time, that special privilege, a rush of guilt washes through my body. Guilt for not wanting to share my son with the world. I don't want him to go through what he was sent to do.

Next, I feel a rush of gratitude that God chose me and Joseph to be his earthly parents. To know him as a baby, a young boy, and now the man that will be the savior.

And then a rush of grace, grace that fills and heals my heart.

Chapter Twenty-Six

Naomi

Goats, I hate them. I stand knee-deep in mud. There's not a clean spot on my scarf to wipe the mud from my face. I hate this job. Why can't Aran pay a servant to feed them? He could, but no, he won't. He says it's good for me, keeps me young.

I trip over another goat as it creeps up behind me looking for a handout, a bite of the grub, they climb over one another to devour. Tending to these dirty, greedy goats is just one of the many chores Aran expects from me. Saying no is not an option. He has even gone as far as telling me to smear mud on my face, so the neighbors won't know it's me doing all the servant's work.

I trudge through the mud, shooing the goats away. There's no more food for them; the basket is empty. Making my way out of the muddy pin, I set the empty basket down looking for a dry spot on the ground to sit and catch my breath.

My mind goes to the conversation Aran and I had earlier today. "Aran, you'd better get going. You have a lot to do before you and Seth leave for Jerusalem. We both know if you don't go now, you will probably get sidetracked and end up drinking too much with your buddies and never get back home before nightfall. So go, get out of here."

Yes, I thought. *Get out of here and never come back.*

As he wobbled to the door, he raised his arm at me as if to say, "Old woman, leave me alone. I will go when I'm good and ready. Don't you have some goats to feed?"

I followed him to the door because I couldn't wait for him to be gone. He left, and I latched the door behind him.

How have I stayed with this man for all these years? Probably to watch over and protect a son from his wretched father. I'm not sure I have been successful at that either.

Anger and a bit of hatred start to consume my mind. I don't want that to happen because I don't want to hate anyone, especially the father of my son. My thoughts drift to a time when Seth was still innocent. I wish for those days again.

Realizing I have been sitting near the goat pen for some time now, I force myself up and brush off as much mud as I can. Some of it crumbles off, but most of it has soaked into the fibers of my clothing. I walk into the house and hear a knock at the front door.

Oh my, I hope it's not Aran back already.

"Okay," I say to the person waiting. "I will be right there."

I open the door, bracing myself for a verbal blast of Aran's anger. But it doesn't come.

"Seth! I'm so glad it's you."

He doesn't answer but gives me the once over. He starts laughing at the mud that clings to me head to toe.

"What's going on? Playing with your goat friends again?"

I laugh and grab a piece of mud off my sleeve and hurl it at Seth, just missing him. "I hate those animals. Come here. Give your mother a big hug." I move toward him acting as if I want to give him a muddy hug.

Seth dances around the furniture, trying his best to stay away. We stop and burst out laughing. I motion for him to sit down. Going into my bedroom I change clothes and attempt to get as much mud off as possible. I return to the main room.

Seth asks, "Didn't Father tell you I had to run some errands and I would be back around midday?"

"No, he didn't. You know your father. He only talks to me when he needs me to do something or if he wants to holler at me for no reason at all."

Seth chuckles. "Sorry, Mother. It's not funny. I'm laughing because he treats me the same way." His expression turns serious. "I'm glad Father isn't here now. I want to talk to you about some things that have happened and what our plans are in Jerusalem."

He leans forward and pulls a clump of mud from my hair. Then he tosses it out the open window.

"I want you to hear it straight from me. I don't want you to find out from anyone else."

My heart flips. "You're making me nervous. What are you up to? And do I want to know? I've lived most of my life with my eyes closed to the ways of your father—and now you. You know that your life is not the life I want for you. I'm so afraid of what might happen to you."

He sighs. "Nothing bad will happen to me, Mother. I want you to know I have—used to have—a girlfriend. Her name is Tabitha. She lives in Sychar."

"Used to have? Why didn't you tell me about Tabitha sooner?"

"I should have. I loved her. I wanted to marry her. I didn't care about her past but—"

"But what?"

"She was like the women you used to warn me against. You called them wild, worldly women, who just wanted what they wanted, when they wanted it, and didn't care how they got it. She was like that until she met someone getting water at the well one day."

"What are you talking about? How did that change her?"

"The last time I went to see Tabitha, she told me about her experience meeting a man at the town's well when she went there for water. She came running home all excited to tell me this man offered her living water, and that she would never thirst again if she truly knew who he was. She told me this man knew everything about her. That she'd had many husbands and boyfriends, and that the man with her now—me—was not her husband. He had many details of her life. Details only she knew."

"Who? Who was the man?"

"Mother, it was Jesus."

"Jesus! Is she sure it was him? Maybe she heard the name wrong."

"No, Mother, it was Jesus. She told me Jesus held out his hands in front of her and water filled his cupped hands and overflowed onto the ground. He told her, 'The water I give gushes fountains of endless life.' Mother, her life now gushes. It's overflowing with the love and belief in all that Jesus says and does."

"So, is that the reason you two are no longer together? You don't have the same belief she has?"

"Well, I don't have the belief she has, that's for sure. But I still love her. Together we have seen Jesus do things I can't explain. It makes my head spin, but Father is there to stop that as fast as possible. He is one stone-cold, hard man."

"You don't have to tell me. I believe his heart is made of cold stone, never to be chiseled away. But you, Seth—you still have a chance to break through the stone."

He shakes his head and stares at his feet. "Mother, you don't understand. It's too late for someone like me. My sins are too much, too big. I can't do enough to receive the living water Jesus is offering. I would have to live a thousand lives working, doing enough to even come close to paying for the sins of my life. It could never be enough."

"Seth, isn't that what Jesus is trying to tell us? We can't do it ourselves. We need a savior for our sins. I have heard Jesus say this myself. Don't tell your father, but I have gone to hear him speak. I have dressed like an old woman with a cane and a veil covering my face. Your father could walk right past me and not recognize me. As a matter of fact, he has. Jesus wants us to trust in him for all the *enoughs* we can never do. To seek forgiveness, for life everlasting with him when our earthly life is no more. There is more—much more—I believe he wants us to be with him someday in his heaven."

Seth continues to look down at the floor, neither one of us saying a word. Then Seth looks up and whispers, "There is no forgiveness for what I am about to do. My trip to Jerusalem is to stop Jesus from carrying on with his ministry. I have to help Father and others shut him down and shut him up. He will be going away for a long time. He will have plenty of time to forget his story sitting in prison. Soon people will forget about him and what he is telling them. That is the reason Tabitha and I are no longer together. We aren't on the same side of belief."

"So, you and your father and these others are going to what? Conspire to have Jesus arrested and thrown in jail for his teachings?"

"Yes, that's the way I understand it from Father. We are going to be heroes, and everybody will know how important we were in stopping what Jesus calls the Good News from confusing and disrupting the masses of the people. We'll be keeping a revolt from taking place against the high priests and high officials. We will be forever known as the ones to help stop the lies from being shared generation after generation."

He leans forward and looks into my eyes, seeking approval. "Mother," he says, "this is an opportunity for Father and me to make a name for ourselves. This is bigger than petty robbery or even a great heist. We can live legitimate lives working for governors, kings, or high officials. We will have more riches than gold and silver. We will have respect and power. It will set us free."

I can't agree with him. Knowing there is nothing more I

can say, I take Seth in my arms. My mind immediately goes to the woman who has been like an angel on earth to me. My eyes fill with tears as I remember Mary saying to me, "Naomi, yes, we want to protect, carry the burdens of our sons, take the arrows of life's madness and sadness for them, but we can't. We must trust in a power greater than us, to watch over them. Pray to God for strength. We must give our life fully and freely to God and trust in him that our sins will be forgiven, provided for."

Part Three   Open Your Eyes

Chapter Twenty-Seven

Seth

Bright and early Father and I are on the road, trying our best to keep up with Jesus. But we're also trying to stay out of sight. We have inserted ourselves in a caravan of people—some followers of Jesus, some merely on their way to Jerusalem—who are selling their wares at the upcoming Festival of the Passover.

People make a lot of money during this time, some of it honest, some of it not. Over the years, Father and I have taken our fair share of money from travelers during the Passover. Some years the profit was much better than others. That thought takes me back to the time about eighteen years ago when we made the great heist of our lifetime. Or so we thought at the time.

When we got back home from robbing the temple treasury, we discovered, with great surprise and disappointment, that most of the bags were not filled with the silver and gold coins we were hoping for. No, they were filled with worthless pieces of tin. To this day, we are still not sure who stored tin there. It's not something I bring up much since Father is still bitter about it. What we got away with after the split with the others was barely enough to replace the donkey that died of exhaustion from the getaway trip back home.

It makes me smile just a little when I think about the

expression on Father's face when he looked into the bags and saw the dull surface of the metal, not the shiny, stunning glare of gold and silver coins.

With my mind a million miles away, I'm shaken back to reality when a voice yells in my direction. Jesus and some of his disciples have stopped and stepped aside from the moving caravan so Father and I can hear him say, "Seth, hey, it's okay, you can come out in the open. You and your father don't have to hide or sneak around any longer. I know what you guys are up to. We all have a job to do on this journey. I hope the wages you and your father are getting are worth all your troubles. Let me make it easier for you. Why don't you come on up here with me so you two can see up close what's going on? It's about to get exciting. Isn't it interesting how your life's path has put you by my side until the very end?"

I try not to make eye contact with Jesus as Father and I move methodically and slowly over the dusty roads. We follow the backs of those in front of us, trusting they are following the person in front of them, who is ultimately following Jesus.

When we get closer, Jesus smiles. "Seth, Aran," he says, "it's good to see you made it. Please introduce yourselves to my disciples as we walk on. Aran, the man to your right is Judas. Judas meet Aran. I know you two already have something in common. You both like money. Judas is the keeper of our money box. He knows what goes in and comes out. One could say he loves it more than anything else. Am I right, Judas?"

Judas looks down at the wooden box clutched tightly under his arm. He mutters, "I'm just trying to look out for your best interest."

Father hesitates to acknowledge the man, but then Judas stretches out his hand to Father. "Aran, it is good to meet you," Judas says casually.

"Nice to meet you, Judas."

As they continue their greeting, Father looks very uneasy. I'm not sure why.

Sometime later, as we near Sychar, Tabitha's hometown, my heart skips a beat. I wonder if I will see her. I hope so.

A voice off in the distance interrupts my daydreaming. "Master, Jesus, have mercy on us!"

Jesus stops. Everyone looks in the direction of the shouting, which is coming from behind a group of bushes.

There's more than one. Several men crouch behind the bushes. Scared, not wanting the people walking by to see them.

Not even thick bushes can hide what I see. The deadly lesions of leprosy. The disease is laced all over their exposed skin. Their faces, deformed with ulcers, are disfigured. Some have stumps at the end of their arms where their hands used to be. It is horrifying. They are society's outcasts. The walking dead.

Strict laws quarantine lepers away from healthy people so they don't spread the disease. The law forces them to ring a bell and shout "unclean" any time people approach them. Being fifty yards away is too close for me.

Jesus tells the man and the others with him, "Show yourselves to the priests."

I can't believe my eyes when, one by one, the men come out from behind the bushes. Some people in our group run away. Father grabs my arm and tries to pull me with him as he takes off running. I shake off his hold, and he disappears into the crowd.

As the lepers show themselves, I gasp. Their skin looks healthy. Their ulcers and lesions—all are gone, healed. My heart races when I look at each man's hands. Their fingers are restored as if they never had the terrible, deforming disease.

Jesus turns and walks down the road when one man runs up to him and falls at Jesus' feet. He thanks him again and again for what he has just done.

Jesus looks down at the healed man. "Were there not more of you cleansed? Where are they now? Are you the only one who came to me giving glory to God? Stand up and go; your faith has healed and saved you."

This man does not miss a beat. He jumps up and runs off in front of us with healed arms and ten fingers pointing high in the air. "I'm healed!" he shouts. I'm saved! Thank you, Jesus! Thank you, Jesus!"

I look at Jesus, and he looks at me.

"Seth, where is Aran?" he asks.

I scan the crowd, looking for Father, but he is nowhere to be found. Judas, who had been walking close to Jesus, is now nowhere to be seen either. I resume walking with Jesus, listening as his followers sing hymns quietly behind us.

Chapter Twenty-Eight

Aran

My heart is pounding so fast, I feel it pushing against my chest. I'm afraid it might burst. I must stop to put both my hands on my knees and lean over to catch my breath. It takes all I have to stop the shaking.

After seeing all those people with leprosy, the last thing I want to do is stick around and chitchat with them like Jesus is doing. That's scary. Some of my friends who attended scripture readings at the temple stopped going because of people like them. Once they heard about leprosy, many stayed away. *How do we know who has leprosy or not?* The risk was greater than their faith, I guess. I don't blame them. I wouldn't want to take a chance of getting exposed to something that might kill me. I might never get leprosy, but why take the chance?

A tap on my shoulder startles me back into an upright position. I turn to see Judas. "Aran," he says, "come with me. We must hurry before someone sees us together."

Even though my breath is still ragged, I follow Judas. He carries the wooden box under his arm. Around the bend is a man sitting on a camel, holding the reins of two more beasts. I hope these two camels are for us. Yes, Judas takes one and motions for me to get on the other. With great effort and help from Judas, I throw my short stub of a leg over the top of the camel, and off we go, bouncing down the road.

I have only ridden a camel a time or two. I do everything I can to stay on this stinky animal. It's a very uncomfortable ride, but it's much better than walking. The nonstop, rhythmic ride of the galloping camels gets us to Jerusalem faster than I have ever traveled before. If we were on foot, the twenty-plus miles we traveled would have taken us at least ten hours longer. When all this is over, I will buy a camel. No more walking for me.

We stop at the temple square. Judas slides down the side of his camel, walks over to the unknown man, who remains atop his camel. They talk, and Judas reaches into the wooden box and pulls out two silver coins.

After I slide (more like roll) off my camel, the mystery rider—who never turns around—holds the reins of all three camels in his hand and then kicks the sides of his camel. All three camels head away from the Square.

I follow Judas over to a side door of the temple. The door faces toward the back, hidden, so if you don't know it's there, you wouldn't even know it exists. Judas looks around to make sure no one sees us, then he knocks on the door. He reminds me of a rat crawling around, trying to sneak in where it's not supposed to.

"Who is it?" a voice asks from the other side of the door.

"It's me, Judas. They're expecting me."

"Who's expecting you?"

Judas seems a bit agitated and eager to be on the other side of the door. He says curtly, "Saul and the Chief Priest. Now let me in."

The door creaks and cracks as it slowly opens. A short man, who is even rounder than I am, motions for Judas and me to follow him. It is a dark, narrow walkway lined with small candles every twenty feet. When we reach the end of the walkway, there is an open door. It's a tall and thick wood door, leading into a dark, musty-smelling round room. It's lit by a stream of light that filters through the window.

Our escort points inside the room and tells us—not

invites us—to go in and sit at a large round table in the middle of the room. As Judas thanks the man, the door we passed through closes.

I move deeper inside the room. The table and its matching chairs are made from fine wood and ornately carved. In front of us stands a wide and tall cabinet with miscellaneous artifacts placed elegantly on the shelves. Some of the ornate vases and sculptures of priests long gone would be worth a lot of money. I think about taking one, but then decide it might be too risky with Judas right there.

Judas and I each pull out a large chair from the table and sit down. Placing the wood box on the table with his hands clutched around both sides, he rests it against his chest. If anyone thinks they can separate Judas from his box, they'd better think again.

I soon feel the room's floor vibrating under my feet. The vases in the cabinets jiggle slightly. The movement separates the cabinet vertically in the middle. Two men step through the secret passageway. Robes cover them head to toe, which makes an effective disguise. I do not know who they are. They sit in the chairs opposite us. They offer no introductions, so I'm not sure whether it is Saul and the Chief Priest across the table.

A voice breaks the silence. "Judas, Aran, thank you for coming. I trust you have had excellent travels."

Before I can respond, Judas sits up taller in his chair and says, "Yes, it was good. Thank you for providing the camels. The trip was much quicker."

The robed man to our right bends his head forward, acknowledging Judas's appreciation.

Then he continues. "The time is near for us to complete our plan. We need to discuss exactly how we are to accomplish it."

Turning his covered face in my direction, the cloaked man says, "Aran, you will give all the information you and your son, Seth, have been gathering against Jesus to the chief priests, and then they will present it to Caiaphas, the High Priest. You and your son will receive your wages shortly after completing your service."

Turning back to Judas, he says, "Because you know where Jesus will be most of the time, we will look to you to signal the place and time of Jesus' arrest. Any thoughts on how you plan to do that?"

Judas relaxes his death grip on the wooden box and raises his right hand toward his head. "Well, yes," he replies. "I have a thought, but before we get too far into the details, I thought it would be good to discuss my reward for my services."

The man nods. "Of course, Judas, I should have known you would want to first discuss your take for betraying Jesus."

For the first time since we sat down, the two robed men turn their heads toward each other. The man on the left leans down to the floor next to him and picks up a small leather pouch. He places the pouch on the table and pushes it to Judas.

Judas's eyes grow wider, and he doesn't hesitate to lean forward to grab the leather pouch mid-push. He first lifts the lid of the wooden box, then opens the pouch and begins dropping something metal into the box. It's that silver-on-silver ping. The chorus of pings stopped at thirty.

After Judas drops the last coin, he looks up at the robed men. With an eerie half-smile, he says, "Thank you. My plan is to simply walk up to Jesus and kiss him on his cheek. At that moment, you should have the guards arrest him."

Again, the two men glare at each other.

"That's it? You are going to just kiss him on his cheek? At what time and place do you plan for this to take place?"

"Yes, I will kiss Jesus so that way all the guards will know exactly which person to arrest. Not everyone has seen Jesus up close. I'm not sure of the time or place at this moment, but when I am, I will tell Aran and Seth. They will let the guards know and set the next events in motion."

The man leading the meeting stands up and proclaims, "It is done. Soon it will be over."

He turns, and the other man, who didn't say a single word, gets up and follows him through the divided cabinet, which slowly becomes one again.

A voice behind us quietly says, "Gentlemen, please follow me."

It is as if a ghost has appeared from nowhere. I hadn't heard the tall, thick door open or any footsteps. He escorts us down the dark hall. The door opens, and the brightness of the sun quickly reminds me I haven't seen it for a while, and it momentarily blinds me. Even though I shield my eyes from the abrupt change, I can see nothing except large white spots floating in front of me.

A voice near me whispers, "I will be in touch soon."

My eyes adjust to the sunlight, and I find myself standing in the temple courtyard alone. Judas is gone, presumably to put our plans into motion. There's no turning back now.

Good, I don't want to turn back. No regrets for me. Seth and I are about to make history, make a name for ourselves. It's about time. It's our time.

Chapter Twenty-Nine

Seth

What if Tabitha and I were married?

That thought keeps bouncing in my head. More than once have I dreamed we were married. That idea doesn't sound half bad to me. Then I do a reality check and figure she will not marry someone who doesn't have the same beliefs she has. It's probably best that people who don't agree on religious stuff don't get married. But maybe I should ask Jesus what he thinks. I sure miss her.

Well, it's been a long, restful day. It was nice to take a much-needed nap or two after spending day after day traveling. I loved not doing anything all day. But the sun is going down fast. I should head over to the house where Jesus is staying to see what, if anything, is going on tonight.

As I approach the house, I change my thoughts from being married to wondering where Father is. Last time I saw him, he was running away as fast as his short fat legs could go. My guess is he ran all the way to Jerusalem. For a man who talks so high and mighty, he is afraid of his own shadow, and apparently of people who don't have perfect skin . . . or are missing limbs.

I near the house in the night's darkness. An arm holding a mug stretches out through a small window. The arm raises the mug in greeting.

"Seth, good evening." It's Jesus's arm and voice. He

motions through the window for me to come in and join him. I head for the door and go inside.

He says, "I trust you had a good day of rest. I have. Please join me and the others for some dinner.".

I walk in and take a place on the floor next to the table, which is covered with plates of food. I haven't eaten all day, and I am starving.

Jesus picks up a piece of bread and asks, "Where is your father? Didn't he return from his great escape from *those people*?"

Embarrassed, I look down at the floor. I say, "I'm not sure where he is. Knowing him, he went on to Jerusalem without me."

"That's okay. My keeper of the ministry money, Judas, is a no-show, too. Who knows? Maybe they traveled together, wanting to make sure our time in Jerusalem will be as it is to be?"

The hair on my arms stood straight up as a chill ran down my spine. Thinking fast, I try to persuade Jesus that Father and I are only going about our business.

"Jesus, you said the other day in the caravan that you know what Father and I are doing by following you. But we just happen to be traveling to Jerusalem, too. We are not up to anything other than business as usual. You know me from way back. We're friends. I wouldn't lie to you. What do you think we are up to?"

I hoped he wouldn't answer.

"Where do I begin? You are right when you say we go way back. I knew then you would follow your father and not the heavenly father. But I say to you, it's still not too late."

A much-welcomed distraction approaches in the form of one of Jesus' followers. He walks over to us and whispers in Jesus' ear. Jesus nods to the man. Then the man walks over to the door and opens it, gesturing to someone to come in.

This newcomer is older and no doubt a man of means. His robe is made from fine linen. It's colorful with intricate designs sewn all over it, from top to bottom. His white beard rests gracefully down on his chest.

"Jesus," the man says, "thank you for letting me in. I can't stay long. The others will wonder where I am."

Jesus nods to affirm his observation. "Yes, your fellow Pharisees would not like it if they knew you were speaking to me alone. They don't like what I have to say. Their self-righteousness is self-serving. Nicodemus, what did you come here for?"

"Rabbi, we know that you have come from God as a teacher because no one can do these signs that you do unless God is with him."

Jesus raises his hand. "You're absolutely right. Unless one is born again, he or she cannot see the kingdom of God."

I look up from my plate. Mid-bite, my mind fires off. What? *Born again?* What is Jesus talking about?

This Nicodemus has the same issues. He asks, "But how can a person be born again? You can't re-enter your mother's womb."

Yes, the man asks the odd but obvious question I have. I put my plate down and turn toward Jesus. He's got my attention now.

"Nicodemus, please listen to me. I say to you unless one is born of water and the Spirit, he or she cannot enter the kingdom of God. That which is born of the flesh is flesh, and that which is born of the Spirit is spirit. You must be born again."

I'm still struggling to follow. I listen harder to Jesus' answer if that's possible.

Jesus says, "The wind blows where it comes from and where it is going; so is everyone who is born of the Spirit. That's the way it is with everyone born from above by the wind of God, the Spirit of God."

Nicodemus is showing signs of frustration now. He leans toward Jesus. "I still wonder how can these things be?"

"Nicodemus, you are a respected teacher of the Jewish

people, and you still don't understand. When I tell you things that are plain as the hand before your face and you don't believe me, what use is there in telling you of the things you can't see, the things of God? Simply this: For God so loved the world that he gave his only begotten Son, that whoever believes in Him shall not perish, but have eternal life."

The world? God loves everyone in the world. Me? Father? My mind is going faster than ever. The older gentleman scans the room, making eye contact with us all, then turns back to Jesus.

"Jesus," he says, "I must go. They will look for me if I don't return soon. Thank you for taking the time to speak with me today. This I promise you: I will always believe in you and urge others to listen with an open and fair loving ear. I just hope they will."

Listening to all that was said, I still can't put all the pieces together. From watching Jesus walk on water, to hearing him tell us we must be born again, I don't know what to think.

But the Pharisee accepted it and believed in what Jesus said. Why can't I?

Jesus hugs Nicodemus goodbye and turns to the rest of us in the house. "We must go first thing in the morning," he says. "There is still a lot to be done."

I reach for my plate of food and pick around what remains, realizing I'm not hungry anymore. I remember the time Jesus told me he knew what Father and I were up to, and it was not too late. Too late for what? Picking a different father to follow or not rat on him? Even if I thought about not turning Jesus in, I know Father would. I don't even think the ultimate threat of death would change Father's mind. I am sure he would stand firm against Jesus until his last breath.

Chapter Thirty

Seth

We're on the road early after last night's visit from Nicodemus. I think again about Father's labored breathing because I'm breathing harder and harder as we travel along a hilly, dusty road that the locals call the Jericho Road. Many groups of people are walking together, chatting as they go along. I'm not sure if Jesus is leading the pack or bringing up the rear. I'm in the middle, neither leading nor following.

I'm confused as to why we are heading to Jericho and not straight to Jerusalem. I recognize the guy who stepped out of the boat, and I consider asking him. I think his name is Peter.

I catch up with the water walker and politely ask, "Excuse me, Peter, can you tell me why it seems we are heading to the town of Jericho and not straight to Jerusalem?"

Peter looks at me with an expression that says he seems to know me, but he hasn't a clue who I am. "Do we know each other?"

"No, I don't think so," I reply.

Maybe he is beginning to suspect something. I will try to settle that if he is. I hope he doesn't recognize me from the boat. I swat at my hair like a bug is near, hoping my hair will cover more of my face. No, I'm just going to be honest.

"My name is Seth. I grew up in Nazareth with Jesus. I

have been traveling around in the shadows with you guys. Remember the night you walked to Jesus on the water? I was a stowaway. At least it looked like you were walking on the water. How did you two do that? Were there rocks or a sandbar underneath you?"

Peter laughs. "Rock! Sandbar! Man, are you crazy? We were out in the middle of the lake, the deepest part of the lake. Yes, I assure you I walked on top—not in—the water. It was only when I heard the wind and saw the waves surround me like angry people trying to attack me that I took my eyes off Jesus and sank. So, yes, that was me. I was the only one who had enough faith to take that step out of the boat."

"Peter, what do you mean by 'had faith'?"

"Well, I trusted Jesus completely, without doubt. I believe Jesus is who he says he is. When Jesus told me to come to him on the water, I knew I could trust him to keep me from drowning. He told me clearly to focus on him and not take my eyes off him. Well, it started out great. I took steps of faith on the water toward Jesus. You even saw it yourself. But what you didn't see was that I took my eyes off him. I thought I needed to do something myself, other than what Jesus told me to do. And then down I started to go. My faith soon became watered down, and that's when the cold waves crept up my legs, trying to take me under, trying to take me from Jesus."

As Peter is reliving this incredible experience, I realize he was definitely on top of the water for quite a few steps. Father can't talk that one away from me. He just wouldn't believe it.

Brushing the hair off my face, I look at him as he continues. "When I cried out to Jesus, he grabbed me immediately. He saved me. I know now more than ever, that if I trust and focus on Jesus in all areas of my life, he will save me. Don't you see, Seth? God has sent Jesus to seek and save all of us. It doesn't matter what the depth of the waters of our life you are trying to navigate is, if you focus your life completely on Jesus, never taking your eyes off him, he will always be there for us, with his hand stretched out to you."

Peter stretches out both of his hands toward me, and without thinking, I almost reach back. I catch myself mid-stretch and quickly adjust my tunic as if it needed to be adjusted.

"Seth, anyone on that boat could have walked out on that water to Jesus if only he had the trust and faith in him to do so. I'm not anyone special. I just took a step of faith out of the boat. What's your boat? The experience I shared with Jesus that night is one that only I can understand. But you can also have those same special moments with Jesus if you trust him and put your faith in him."

Peter stops walking, and I stop alongside him. People wander past us as if we were two rocks on the road.

"Seth, do you remember King Solomon's teachings?"

I know none, but I don't tell him that. "A few," I answer. "Which one are you thinking of?"

"One of the first proverbs written by this wise king was this: 'Trust in the Lord with all your heart and do not lean on your own understanding. In all your ways acknowledge him, and he will make your paths straight. Do not be wise in your own eyes; Fear the Lord and turn away from evil.'"

I motion for Peter to go on and make his point as we begin to walk again.

"Seth," he asks, "don't you get what I'm saying? It goes back to the eyes." He points at his eyes with the first and second fingers of his right hand. "When I took my eyes off Jesus after he told me not to, I sank, drowning in my own understanding."

Irony floods my mind. That is the exact opposite of what my father has told me since I was a boy. Father told me to be your own man. Do what you want to do. Trust in yourself and nobody else. Life is all about you, and what you want.

As I think about the two different paths of life, I feel myself gasping for air as if I am sinking, drowning in this huge lake of life.

Catching my breath, I can't believe what I am about to say. "Peter, I know you have faith in Jesus, that you are someone special, one of Jesus' followers. But I am nothing like that. I'm just a conman, a thief, a man living a life for my selfish pleasures. Life is short, and I'm out to get as much as I can, live the way I want to. Why should Jesus care about me? Or care if I believe in him or that I am a sinner? I'm not worth spending time on."

Peter spins around and looks me straight in the eyes.

"Seth, I'm no one special. I'm just a fisherman with a hot temper from time to time. I could talk using vulgar language if I wanted to."

For a moment, that's what I thought he was about to do.

"The only education I got was from the school of hard knocks. If you think I am a man without sin, pure and clean, you are sorely mistaken. If you want to compare sins, I can put mine up against anyone else's, and you will see I'm no different from any other person. It makes no difference if you are only a light sinner or a sinner on a mission—sin is sin. There is no one without sin, no one perfect, except for one."

Taking a few quick steps, I widen the space between me and Peter. "You're going to tell me it's Jesus, right? I remember growing up with him. He was this perfect little boy that all mothers wanted their sons to be like. I never saw him do anything wrong then, and I haven't seen him do anything wrong now. He's Mr. Perfect."

I ended my little jab with sarcasm and heavy frustration.

Peter takes a step toward me. I squint, not wanting to see the punch coming my way. But he hits me only with words, calmly saying, "Seth, open your eyes. See what I have seen."

Then this blurry figure turns and walks away.

Chapter Thirty-One

Seth

It must be getting close to dinnertime because my stomach is rumbling. It has been a long walk on the Jericho Road, but talking with Peter helped pass the time. Our conversation has gone from intense to eerily silent. It looks as if he is now talking to himself. I see his lips move, and now and then, he raises his hands over his head and waves them toward the clouds.

As we round a bend, the road slopes, making the downhill walk much more inviting than the climb up. I notice a man up ahead. He's sitting on the side of the road, shouting, trying to get the attention of the people.

But everyone keeps passing him right on by. To my surprise, Jesus comes up behind me and Peter. He eases us apart, walks between us, and moves into the lead. Jesus seems interested in who this man is because he looks toward the source of the shouts.

I pick up my pace to stay close to Jesus. My nosiness has me curious. I want to know who this man is and what Jesus will do, if anything. If something happens, I want to be right there to see it—no more hiding for me.

Peter catches up to us and says, "Jesus, I will walk ahead and make sure that man yelling out to the passersby doesn't bother you."

Jesus reaches out and grabs hold of Peter's right arm and

replies, "No, Peter. Let's see what he wants. He's asking people about me and seems eager to talk to me. I want to hear what he has to say."

With a frown bordering on a scowl, Peter raises his arm, breaking the hold Jesus has on him. "I'm just thinking about your time. If we stopped for everyone seeking a conversation with you, we would never get to our destination. Plus," Peter points one hand toward the sky, "it's getting late, and people are going to want to stop and have dinner soon. Jericho is only about a half-mile walk from here."

"Peter, if you're that hungry, walk on. I will be right behind you."

As Jesus returns his focus toward the man, who is now only about twenty feet from us, Peter drops his hand in exasperation.

Jesus and I near the man on the side of the road, and I can see his expression. His eyes are wide open, but he appears unable to see a thing.

Jesus stops in front of the man.

The man cries out, "Jesus! Son of David! Have mercy on me!"

"What do you want me to do for you?" Jesus asks.

The man reaches toward the voice in front of him and finds Jesus' forearms. He takes hold of them and says, "Lord, I want to regain my sight! I want to see again!"

"Go ahead," Jesus answers. "See again. Receive your sight. Your faith has saved and healed you."

The blind man immediately shouts, "I can see! I can see!"

Everyone standing around, including impatient Peter, begins shouting praise to God. Peter raises his hands to the sky.

I just stand there, blinded by the lack of my own belief. How can this man now see because Jesus told him, "Go ahead see. Your faith has saved and healed you"? What was he talking about? Maybe this so-called miracle was planned.

How do I know this man wasn't a plant and not really blind? Now I'm thinking like Father. Like I should. This is nothing more than a trick.

While walking that last stretch of the road to Jericho, the singing and shouting of praises never stops. The crowd walking with Jesus presses in on him more and more. As we enter the city, the man whose sight supposedly had been restored struggles his way back through the crowd toward Jesus. He points at a tree, and excitedly says, "Jesus, look. There is a man up in that tree. He must be trying to see you as you walk past."

I turn to see for myself. Yes, there is a man who is the approximate height of a ten-year-old boy holding on for dear life midway up a sycamore tree. It is pretty funny to see him—a well-dressed, older man—clinging to the tree. Jesus is now within shouting distance. He looks up at the man in the tree and says, "Zacchaeus, hurry and come down. Today I must stay at your house."

Does Jesus know this strange man in the sycamore? I've got to get myself into this man's house tonight to see what happens.

The little man can't get down out of the tree fast enough. In a whirl of excitement, he runs over to Jesus. "Jesus," he says, "I would gladly have you as my guest in my home. I will have a great meal prepared for you."

"Thank you, Zacchaeus. You should invite some of your friends too. If it is okay with you, I will have a couple of my disciples join us as well as this gentleman."

Jesus points at me.

Yes! I'm in!

Zacchaeus's house is beautiful. The finest carved furniture from around the world graces the rooms. The entire grounds and house state the owner is a person of wealth, wanting for nothing. Fine paintings grace every wall; marble statues line the hallways; gold and silver decorated vases fill room after room.

This small man named Zacchaeus escorts us to a large room with a grand table lined with beautiful cushions. "Please, everyone, be seated."

One by one, we recline on the cushions around the table.

After being seated, I lean over and ask Peter. "Who is this guy? Where did he get his great wealth from?"

Peter picks up his wine goblet, takes a small sip, and then holds it out in front of his lips as if to shield what he is about to say. "His title is Chief Tax Collector, also known as the Chief Tax Thief, cheating as many as possible out of their money so he can line his walls with marble statues and his pockets with gold and silver coins."

Chief Thief? He hasn't met Father.

"Well, Peter, any chance he can get me a job" Trying not to laugh too loud.

"I'm not sure why Jesus wanted to come here tonight. The people are wondering why would Jesus agree to be a guest of a crook, a chief sinner." Peter motions with his goblet. "Plus, just look around this table. Other tax collectors, no better than Zacchaeus, are here gawking. See that man over there?"

Without being noticed, we glance at the man sitting on Jesus's right. "That man there is in the business of offering women to men for money. The man next to him sells scales to vendors in the market that tip the scales in the wrong direction if you know what I mean. I can go on and on, but you see what I am talking about. And here sits Jesus in the middle of them as if they are his best friends."

As I look around the table, I recognize some people. Over the years, Father and I had business arrangements with a few of them. Yes, I am surprised to see Jesus having a meal with this kind of people. Although I am "this kind" of person, Jesus still makes time to talk to me.

As our dinner is finishing, one servant enters the grand dining room with a sense of urgency. She goes up to Zacchaeus and whispers something in his ear. Zacchaeus shakes his head.

Then, with no announcement, three men push past the servants and enter the dining room. They seem determined to make an announcement, eager to speak.

Before they can say a word, Jesus raises his arm in their direction and says, "Gentleman, what do you want?"

The man standing between the other two steps forward. "Jesus, care to tell us why you are having this fancy gala in Zacchaeus's home? Don't you know who these people are?" The man waved his arm, motioning to the guests. "Why do you choose to spend your time socializing with sinners?"

Jesus stands and looks around the table. He takes a moment to acknowledge each one of us and then addresses the three men. "Well, teachers of the law, it is not the healthy who need a doctor, but the sick. I have not come to call the righteous, but sinners. Please, come join us. There's room for more."

The spokesperson for the three turns abruptly and walks out. The other two follow, not missing a step.

As Jesus takes his seat, Zacchaeus stands up, and, looking straight at Jesus, says, "Lord, half of my possessions I will give to the poor, and if I have defrauded anyone of anything, I will give back four times as much."

Jesus smiles and nods in acceptance of what the man pledged.

Several others lumber off their cushion. They don't say a word, and, with heads looking down, turn and leave the room.

Jesus lifts his hands toward Zacchaeus and says, "Zacchaeus, today salvation has come to this house. For the Son of man has come to seek and to save that which was lost."

Did I hear that right? Did this Chief Tax Collector—Chief Tax Thief—just pledge to give half of all he has to the poor and pay back four times what he took from others? Good thing my father isn't here. He would call this man a crazy lunatic. I'm questioning Zacchaeus's sanity, too. I'm not the only one either. Most of the guests who are left mumble among one another and get to their feet. They're not wasting a moment to leave. Maybe they're afraid that if they stick around, they might do something stupid, like committing to giving their ill-gotten gains back to those they stole from.

As the table empties, Jesus looks at Peter and the other two disciples. "Gentlemen, we should be going. We need to leave for Jerusalem first thing in the morning."

Next, he turns to me and says, "Seth, I guess you will go with us as well. I'm sure your father is eager to reconnect with you in Jerusalem so you two can finish your job. You are almost done, Seth. It's almost over."

Jesus embraces Zacchaeus as we leave.

Chapter Thirty-Two

Seth

Dead to the world I feel a kick to my feet, which are wrapped in my sleep mat. Then another kick. This time it's a little harder.

A voice somewhere above me says, "Wake up, sleepy head. If you're going with us, you better get up and get ready. We are leaving for Jerusalem. The road will get busy with travelers soon, so Jesus is eager to go."

I squint my eyes open, adjusting to the morning light as I see Peter walking away. I would love to roll over for another rooster's crow, but I should prepare myself for a long day. The smell of fresh bread gives me reason to get up. I don't want to head down the road without filling my stomach first. We have a ways to go today before getting to Jerusalem.

With all the traveling I have done over the years, I'm good at juggling my breakfast and knapsack at the same time. While carrying two large rolls in one hand and an apple in the other the call from Peter goes out to the group. "It's time to go."

After a morning of walking, we finally rested at a place called Mount of Olives. From here it should be a short walk into Jerusalem. I feel relieved we're getting closer to our final destination.

I notice Jesus leaving the group and heading toward the

local temple. I follow him inside. Jesus finds a nice resting place to sit. Unnoticed, I grab the open space behind him and to his right. It is a welcome relief from the walk since the day is heating up.

No sooner do we catch our breaths when in come some of the religious teachers and Pharisees. One man is leading a woman by the back of her neck. I can tell his grasp is hurting her. She is groaning as he throws her toward Jesus. The woman stumbles and falls to her knees. She keeps her head down, her tangled hair covering her face. But it does nothing to cover the sound of her sobs. She is crying so hard she struggles to catch her breath.

Another man steps out from behind the first brute. With a smug look on his face, he says, "Jesus, great teacher among us, I bring to you this wretched woman who was caught in the act of being intimate with a man who is not her husband. Doesn't the law given to us by Moses give us the right to stone this sinful woman to death? What do you have to say about this situation we have brought before you?"

Even I feel uneasy for Jesus. It is obvious these men brought this woman to trip him up, trap him, and accuse him of anything they can to use against him. How is Jesus going to handle this? The case against her seems closed. Those who brought her here agree. They walked in with stones in their hands. Stones that are the perfect size to inflict injury, no death. These men are anxiously waiting for the moment when they can pummel her body. That's how sure they are that there is no other answer to their question.

As I sit there with these thoughts bouncing around in my head, I think maybe Father is right. Maybe Jesus isn't who he says he is. Jesus is no different from anyone else. That would be such a relief to me. I don't have to feel guilty for my life like I have from time to time since traveling with him. I can be me, just me.

Jesus rises from the stone bench. He stands in front of the accusers and reaches down to the woman kneeling before him. He brushes her hair from her face.

Suddenly Jesus drops to his knees. He writes in the dirt with his finger. As he does, the religious leaders shout in anger, "She should die right? We have the right to stone her. The law says so. She has sinned. She must be put to death. She must pay for her sins!"

After some time passes, Jesus stands up, patting his hands together to knock off the dust. The crowd is ready to rain down their stones on this woman.

He says, "Any one of you without sin, go ahead and throw your stone at this woman."

One by one, they look down at what Jesus has written. With their heads bowed, I hear thud, thud, thud as the men drop stone after stone to the ground.

It is amazing to see this large procession of people walk away. Not a word is uttered. After the last one is out of the temple, Jesus reaches down, takes the woman by the arm, and helps her to her feet. She stands before him shaking, still waiting for her body to be beaten and broken by the rocks selected for her.

Jesus pulls back her hair that is covering her eyes. "Look around. Where are those who would condemn you? Are there any here?"

With a look of shock on her tear-stained and dirty face, she looks around, making a complete circle. "No one, Master," she says.

"Then neither do I. Go now and leave your life of sin."

She turns and runs out of the temple. Like her, I am shocked she is able to live another day. Yes, Jesus saved this woman from a certain death by writing something in the dirt. I can't see the writing from here, so I make my way over to it.

But as I approach, Jesus swishes the dirt with his foot, creating a small dust cloud. I can still see the faint outlines of names written in the dirt before it is all gone.

Among the names, I see two that grab my attention: Seth

and Aran.

Jesus notices me behind him, turns, and walks away without saying a word. Peter shows up about that time.

"Peter, why didn't they stone her?" I ask. "She was guilty, caught in the act. Why wasn't she stoned to death?"

"You're right, Seth. She is a sinner. But so are the ones pointing their fingers at her. Jesus was simply pointing out we are all sinners deserving to have stones thrown at us. He reminded them they were sinners just like her. There aren't enough stones to kill all the sinners of this world. Truth is, every single one of us has a stone with our name on it.

Peter heads out of the temple. I am the only one left, or so I thought, but then a voice comes out of a dark corner.

"Seth, it's me." I rush toward Father who says, "I wanted to meet up with you before you go to Jerusalem. I want to share the plans about what will happen once Jesus arrives in Jerusalem."

"I have so much to tell you. Father, you don't have to hide in the shadows anymore. Jesus knows we have been following him. As a matter of fact, he has made sure I see and hear everything he does. I travel with him like his closest followers do. I'm almost like them."

Father steps out from behind the marble column. "No! You'd better not be like them. Don't get too chummy with them. We still have an important job to do, and you can't mess it up. Stay focused."

Using the streak of light shining through the small temple window where Father is standing, I look down and see a large stone lying on the ground. I look at Father. "That stone." I point at it. "Were you going to throw it at that woman?"

"Yes."

Not saying another word, I turn and leave.

In silence, Father follows me out of the temple, and we find a secluded place among the trees. I stand there with my arms folded and my head cocked to one side. "Okay," I say, "what's the plan for when we get to Jerusalem?"

"The plan is really simple. Easy money. We must continue to watch Jesus, stay close to him, and find out what he is going to do before he does it. When we see the best opportunity for Jesus to be taken under arrest by the Roman guards, we will notify the Roman officers from the chief priests."

I look up at Father and whip the hair out of my eyes. "I got it. So far it sounds pretty simple."

"It is."

Father grabs both my arms and looks up, straight into my eyes.

"Seth, as I have said all along, easy money on the road to fame and fortune. Let me finish. Judas will identify Jesus by kissing him on his cheek so the Roman guards will know who to arrest. It's that easy. Once they arrest Jesus, our job is done."

With both my arms still in his grasp, I think another special father-son moment is going to happen. No sooner do I think that when Father pushes me away.

"We will be free to do whatever we want from that point on. Once our new friends in high places pay us, we will be set for life."

I slowly straighten my head and glance off in the other direction, dropping my arms by my side. I don't hear a hint of remorse or second thoughts from Father.

"Are you sure what we are doing is the right choice?" I ask him.

"Right choice! Boy, are you questioning me? After all I have done to get us to this position in our lives, now you're asking me if this is the right choice!"

I have seen Father angry many times, but the darkness in his eyes and the grimace on his face are expressions I have never seen before. It looks as if something else has taken over his body.

"Sorry, Father, this is the right thing to do. It's the right choice for us."

The tug-of-war between yes and no, right and wrong, will not stand in the way any longer. Father and I must complete the plan. Jesus' plan.

Chapter Thirty-Three

Seth

With full resolve to continue helping Father trap Jesus, I bid him safe travels on his way to Jerusalem. I return to where Jesus is staying with his disciples so I can travel with them. For the first time in several weeks, I have a revived energy in what Father and I are doing. I feel a sense of purpose. I see the path set before us now. I am ready to go.

"Jesus is ready to go," shouts Peter.

The disciples and Jesus gather their things and head for the road to Jerusalem. After walking about a half mile, I work my way up the caravan to where Jesus is.

That's odd. Jesus is riding on the back of a young donkey.

This is the first time I've seen Jesus ride any beast throughout his travels. We continue walking some distance. Then the road leads off the Mount of Olives. In unison, the crowd walking with Jesus sing: "Blessed is the king who comes in the name of the Lord. Peace in heaven and glory in the highest!" Many lay down their coats as others place palm branches on the road as Jesus passes through.

As we continue walking, the city of Jerusalem comes into view. It looks beautiful sitting on a hill in the distance. Looking at it and listening to the crowd sing begins to stir up some emotions in me that I can't explain. His follower's commitment to him is like none I have ever seen before.

I try to snap out of this mind game by reminding myself of the pledge to stand firm with Father. To do what we've agreed on needs to be done. I shake off those silly feelings of whatever they are, and I turn my attention to Jesus. Yes, I was moved but not like Jesus, I see tears rolling down his face.

As we get closer to the city, it's clear that many stand in awe of Jesus and then there are those who can't stand him. There is a different presence in the city this time. It's difficult to explain, but I can feel it in my bones. A chill runs up my spine as I walk next to the donkey carrying Jesus through the city's gates on this warm day.

Peter helps Jesus dismount the donkey. They have a short conversation. Jesus does most of the talking, and then he heads down the street to the right.

I walk over to Peter. "Where is Jesus off to now?" I ask.

"He wants to go to the temple and pray. That's never a bad thing. Matter of fact, Jesus has told me more than once I should pray more, talk less."

Peter chuckles as he pats me on my back. "How about you pray for me, and I will pray for you." He slaps my back one more time before walking away.

No thanks, I don't need or want anyone praying for me.

I guess it's good Peter hasn't figured out that I'm following Jesus for a whole different reason than he is. His offer made me think back to when Mother told me she would pray for me. Why do they want to pray for me? If one more person tells me, they will pray for me I will explode. I don't want anyone speaking nonsense to some invisible god for me. If prayer were real, maybe when I was growing up, I wouldn't have been beaten so much by my *loving* father. No god heard my cries for help and came to save me. I can feel my sadness turning into anger, a bit of rage was building up inside me. I need to calm down. I'm sure Jesus has never gotten angry before. I guess that's another thing that makes us different.

Perfect timing, I settle down the angry feelings within me as Jesus stops in front of the temple. I make sure to stay back just enough to not be seen but close enough to see and hear what's going on. I am getting pretty good at it by now. But I don't think Jesus cares anyway.

Jesus stands in front of the main temple entrance and looks left to right, as vendor after vendor lines up with their carts around the temple. The vendors try to shout over each other, each hoping to outsell the competition.

Carts sitting side by side overflowing with pigeons and doves, and money changers changing currency for those wanting to give their tithes and offerings. Or, wanting to buy the next miracle God has to offer.

There were carts filled with merchandise advertised as such to help the temple goer have a more special experience. Vendors promise buyers if they buy doves or pigeons from them, their sins will be forgiven even more than the vendor next to them. Jugs of healing water were being offered for a low, low price, with guarantees assured. It was a crazy, loud madhouse instead of a house of God. Even I knew the temple was not supposed to look like this. This looked no different than the crowded marketplace where making a denarius or two was the goal. The purpose of this place was to make as much money as possible at the cost of religion. It looked like a place of business, not a place of prayer.

Without saying a word, Jesus runs up to a cart filled with pigeons, and with one swift movement, he grabs the bottom and overturns it. Pigeons tumble out of their cages. Feathers fly and birds squawk. Jesus methodically turns cart after cart, causing all the vendors' merchandise to crash to the ground.

Birds and animals scamper away in their newfound freedom. The dirt turns dark from the jugs of water spilled onto the ground.

Whoa. Yes, Jesus can get angry.

The vendors are just as shocked as I am. Not a word is

said when Jesus stands at the temple entrance and cries out, "My house was designated a house of prayer for the nations; You've turned it into a hangout for thieves."

I sense someone walking up behind me. A familiar voice says, "See, Seth, this is the very reason he must be stopped. He must be stopped from doing crazy things, telling people the temple is his house. The chief priests are growing concerned that more people are going to believe Jesus. That can't happen."

"Father, yes, I do see more and more people follow after Jesus. There is definitely a movement growing in that direction. How much longer do you think it will be before they arrest Jesus?"

"Not long. We need more than ever now to watch his every move. They are counting on us."

"And, Father, you can count on me."

Chapter Thirty-Four

Seth

Father leaves and I look around the temple for Jesus. I don't see him. Then a tap on my shoulder startles me. I turn around. "Tabitha! I am so glad to see you!"

Putting my arms around her, I give her a big hug before even asking if it is okay. Thankfully, she hugs me back.

"Seth, how are you doing?"

"Great, I'm great. Tell me what you have been up to. Been in Jerusalem very long?"

I am so excited to see her I talk too fast, firing question after question at her. We make our way over to a stone bench under a tree just outside the temple entrance and sit down.

"Were you here when Jesus tossed all the vendor carts?" I ask. "Did you see how mad he was? I have never seen him angry. That was a first for me."

"Yes, I saw it." Her expression seems withdrawn. "I don't blame him for getting so mad. The vendors have been getting worse and worse about pressuring templegoers to buy their stuff. They're turning something sacred into a shameful business. I agree with Jesus that the temple is a place full of robbers and cheats."

"Well, what about Jesus telling everybody it is 'his' house of prayer? Isn't the temple for anyone who wants to use it?"

"I don't think it is so much about ownership as it is

honoring the Father. It's a place for believers to pray, give their tithes, and build a stronger personal relationship with the heavenly Father. It's a special place. All the time you have spent following Jesus and seeing him perform healings and other miracles hasn't it changed you at all? Has it changed your heart? If not, what must he do to change you?"

"I have seen him do, or supposedly do, amazing things, but I don't think I'm going to change. I'm too far gone. I lived too bad of a life to be accepted as one of you. This is the life I have chosen."

"It's not too late. The reason Jesus is here is to accept us. Accept us for who we are. Remember, I was no angel. The life I was living was not good. I avoided other women in my village so they wouldn't judge me or look down on me because of the way I was living my life. That's how I met Jesus. Don't you remember? He accepted me when I accepted the living water he offered me. It's not too late. There will be a time when it is too late for you, but until you take your last breath, it's not."

Tabitha takes my hands in hers. With tears streaming down her face, she says, "I love you, Seth. Jesus loves you. Jesus wants to offer his grace to you."

I don't say a word as we sit there, hand in hand. In silence, time slips away.

Oblivious to what is going on around us, we suddenly hear what sounds like a bunch of young kids singing or shouting at the top of their lungs. I look at Tabitha and she looks at me as we realize something is going on in the temple.

I jump up, and with Tabitha's arm in my hand, we sprint over to see what's going on. We squeeze our way past the crowd of people standing everywhere and see all these kids—there must be at least fifty, if not more—dancing around and shouting, "Hosanna to David's son!"

The kids keep shouting as Jesus reaches out and, one by one, heals those who are blind. Those who couldn't walk before now strut about shouting praises to Jesus. Many who were sick minutes ago are now healed.

Tabitha stands next to me and has her arms swinging up in the air, singing in unison with the kids. But not everyone is thrilled with what is going on. I feel a hard tug of my robe on the side opposite Tabitha. I think for a moment it is going to be pulled off.

"Listen to me," a voice—Father's voice—says, "the chief priests are furious at what Jesus has done today. Hurling all the vendors' carts, chasing them out, and proclaiming the temple is his house—all those actions have got everyone's attention. And now he has all these snot-nosed kids up in arms shouting nonsense. They are losing patience with Jesus. They want us to move faster in setting Jesus up for his arrest. Whatever you do, don't say a word about our plans."

Father gestures with a head bob toward Tabitha and then slinks out of the room. Tabitha is still singing and swaying with the kids. It doesn't appear she knows Father was even here. That's good. It's hard to say goodbye again to her, so I decide to do what my father always does best—I quietly slip away.

Now all by myself, I find a place to roll out my sleep mat and call it a day. The cool breeze of the night and the clear skies are a welcome sight as I lie on my back with my head cradled in my hands. My mind wanders off in different directions.

What if my life were different? What if I had had a different father? One who loved me or at least acted as if he did. What else could I have done with my life other than become a thief, a robber, a stealer? What if I stopped caring what others might think of me? Do I live up to the world's expectations? Why does it seem as if life is so hard most of the time?

All the what-ifs and the whys start flooding my mind. The stars become blurry as tears fill my eyes and flow down my cheeks. To my surprise, I say out loud, "God, if you are real, show me something so that I will know without a doubt you are who Jesus says you are."

Hoping for a second I will hear a booming voice fall from the stars above telling me exactly what to do, I lie there listening to silence. The only sound I hear is my heart beating louder and faster as I drift off to sleep.

Chapter Thirty-Five

Seth

I wake up feeling the most rested I have felt in a long time. That's odd because I pull a large, jagged stick out from under my side that I must have rolled over on in the middle of the night. Oh well, I'll take it. The last few weeks of traveling with Jesus have been exhausting. Honestly, I'm looking for all this to be over with so I can get back to my normal routine—being a simple thief. Also, I want to stop having conversations with myself and people like Tabitha about Jesus. I look forward to being done with him.

A voice comes from behind the tree. "There you are," Father says. "Get up. I have some updated news to share with you. I talked to Judas, and he told me he and the other disciples were going to celebrate the Passover supper with Jesus. Judas thinks that will probably be the best time to arrest Jesus."

"How did you find me out here?"

"Remember, I'm a spy." Father chuckles, acting like he out-smarted me again.

"I can find anyone. You can't hide from me. Besides, the old farmer told me you were here."

He points down the road toward the farmhouse.

"Now let's go, we need to get back in the city. Jesus is going back to the temple. The ones who hired us want us to be witnesses if he breaks the Sabbath laws. It could help support why he should be arrested. So we need to keep watching him, spying on him."

Father turns and heads back to the city. Not waiting, his stubs of legs are moving at a quick pace away from me. I shake my head wondering why I continue to jump at his every command. After a short jog, I catch up to him. Without even looking to confirm I caught up with him he says, "You know, I can't believe we have never been arrested. After all these years and all the robbing we have done, you'd think the authorities would have caught us by now. But look at us! We're as free as the birds that own the sky."

Father looks up as a flock of birds fly right above his head. My mind immediately goes to how funny it would be if a bird or two needed to . . . shame on me. I can't help holding back a chuckle as I turn away.

I roll up my sleep mat and quickly head for the city. Father huffs and puffs to keep up with me. I am walking fast on purpose, revenge for the many cruel things he did to me.

Jesus is already seated in the temple talking to those sitting around him. I find a few inches between two others on one of the stone benches resting against the wall. Father still grasps for air and takes a seat on the other side of the room.

Good. I didn't want to be next to him anyway. It's about time he takes a dip to wash off the smell of his travels. I feel sorry for those squeezed next to him. His body matches who he is inside—a dirty little man.

Jesus stands up and holds up his hand to quiet the room. Then he gestures toward the back of the room. Two of his disciples step outside the temple door. After a minute of awkward silence, the two men enter assisting a woman. Each man on either side had a hold around her arm, doing all they could to keep her from falling.

She is bent over in pain, moaning and groaning with each small step. Jesus walks over to her and lays his hands on her. "Woman, I free you from your sickness."

She stands straight up, and with tears falling off her face, she praises him.

To my surprise, Jesus turns my direction and asks, "Seth, my childhood friend, don't you know who this woman is?"

It takes me a second, then it all comes back to me. This woman is Ruth, the twelve-year-old girl that Jesus and I played with growing up. She was a great marble player. She won our marbles every time we played. I remember her becoming sick suddenly, and she couldn't do anything because she was in continuous pain. No doctor could help her. This poor girl, now a grown woman, has dealt with this for more than eighteen years. I do know who she is and how sick she was. I can't deny she has been healed even if I wanted to.

Jesus turns and walks back to his seat when one of the temple priests jumps up and shouts, "What are you doing, healing someone on the Sabbath?! You can choose any other day to work, but you did it today of all days."

Others throughout the crowd join in condemning what Jesus has done. My father joins in, and he isn't even Jewish. Father couldn't care less about the Sabbath.

"You who speak against me are frauds, hypocrites. Don't you do some things on the Sabbath? How about when you untie your ox or your donkey and lead them down to the water for their daily drink? Why should this woman, bound with her sickness for eighteen long years, not be released, untied, healed today on the Sabbath?"

Half the crowd seems to support every word Jesus is saying. The other half are so furious with Jesus that you can almost see steam coming out of their ears. If looks could kill, Jesus would be gone by now.

The temple leaders now seem out for blood. Father and I only agreed to help the chief priests arrest him, nothing more. But I wonder if that is all they are planning. My mind goes back to the house where Tabitha and I were hiding under the floor. She said she heard someone talk about killing Jesus. Tabitha also thought the man talking about killing Jesus was my father. I don't believe that it was my father. I still don't believe that's what they want to do. Stop him, yes. Kill him, no.

As the angry crowd grows louder and louder, they move toward Jesus. Peter and two other disciples break through the line, grab Jesus by the arm, and head out the back entrance of the temple.

I jump up and head out the front entrance, racing around the back to catch up with Jesus and what now appears to be his bodyguards. They are moving at a fast pace. My heart pounds faster, causing me to gasp for air. Now I know what Father must have felt like trying to keep up with me. I manage a small grin, as I stay right behind them.

Chapter Thirty-Six

Seth

I manage to catch up to Jesus and his henchmen, and as we get farther away from the angry mob at the temple, his bodyguards revert to simply being his disciples. Slowing down to a steady walk, I slip next to Peter.

"Peter, where is Jesus going?"

"It looks as if he's headed to Simon's house. Simon is a leper, *was* a leper, Jesus knows. It's a safe house for Jesus to get away from those who wish to harm him."

As we approach the front door, it bursts open. This man comes running out and heads straight to Jesus. The two hug each other.

We all go in and settle around a large table filled with dates, pears, peaches, goat cheese, and many other delicious food choices. Around the table's perimeter are loaves of fresh bread. To wash it down, servants provide us with tall goblets of wine.

I'm seated next to Peter. "Peter," I lean in so no one else can hear, "how did Simon know Jesus would stop by today for his midday meal?"

"He didn't. Simon doesn't need notice. From the first time he met Jesus, Simon claimed he is always prepared to be in Jesus' presence again, any time, any day."

I eat more than I should because the food is amazing. By the looks of it, all of us overindulged. The disciples are leaning back in their cushions with their hands either behind their heads or resting on their stomachs. Jesus is reclined on a pillow. He is seemingly taking in the quiet, still hours that have escaped him in recent days.

As time goes by, it feels nice and peaceful. This time no mob is accosting Jesus. But a woman is walking over to him. She is holding the most beautiful alabaster jar I have ever seen. Mother had several ornate jars, but none like this one. Without saying a word, the woman breaks open the jar and pours what looks like some kind of oil over his head. It washes over his eyes and runs down his nose. The powerful smell of expensive perfume hits my nose. I recognize the scent. I tried to buy it for Tabitha, but it was more than I could afford. Even with all my ill-gotten money, I hadn't wanted to spend that much.

Why would this woman want to pour such expensive perfume over Jesus's head? What a waste. I am not the only one who thinks this. Peter jumps up and shouts, "Woman! What are you doing? Why would you waste all that expensive perfume?

Judas joins in with Peter. He says, "We should have sold it and kept the money. Imagine what we could have done with it! We could have helped so many poor people. But not now. You just wasted all of it!"

"Stop," Jesus says. "Let her alone. Why are you giving her such a hard time? She has done something wonderfully meaningful for me."

"But Jesus, she is—"

Jesus holds up his perfume-soaked hand to stop Judas from going on. "You will have the poor with you every day for the rest of your lives. But you will not always have me. She did what she could now. By pouring this perfume over me she has anointed my body for burial."

Peter objects to his statement. "Burial? Jesus, what are you talking about? You aren't dying."

"Peter, truly I say to you, wherever the gospel is

preached in the whole world, what this woman has done will also be spoken of in memory of her."

Jesus then talks to all of us. "Now, men, evening is coming. We should go and share one last Passover together." He nods to Peter and John. "You two go into the city. A man will meet you carrying a pitcher of water. Follow him. Whatever house he takes you to, tell the owner of the house, 'Teacher says, where is my guest room in which I may eat the Passover supper with my disciples?' He will show you a large upper room furnished and ready for us. Then after supper, I will want to spend some time in the garden."

I lean toward Peter and quietly ask, "What garden? Why does Jesus want to go to a garden?"

"It's the Garden of Gethsemane, one of his favorite places. He likes to connect to his Father there."

"His Father?"

"Yes, when Jesus wants to get away from everything, the crowds, the craziness of the world, he comes to the Garden of Gethsemane. He prays, rests, gives thanks, and spends time with his heavenly Father by himself. We all need a Gethsemane, Seth. What's yours?"

I think about it and realize I don't have one. Why would I need a place to pray? I don't have a god. My father is no god. Maybe in his mind. No . . . no Garden of Gethsemane for me.

Part Four

It Is Time

Chapter-Thirty-Seven

Seth

The sun is done for the day. The bright light of the moon takes over. Jesus and his disciples walk through the streets of Jerusalem, passing the crowded houses and shops. I'm bringing up the tail end of the line.

Peter stops and stands in front of a two-story house. We all head toward this simple home nestled in between a row of houses that look quite ordinary, certainly nothing fancy.

As we get closer, Judas takes me by the arm and leads me to a stone wall between two houses, separating us from the main crowd. Not sure what Judas is up to, I go along.

"Seth, tonight is the night."

"Night for what?"

"I need you to tell your father that we are going to have Jesus arrested tonight."

I feel my body go numb for a second. This is happening.

"Aran is waiting for my word to implement the plan. He is at the Sheep Gate behind the royal court. He is supposed to gather the guards and lead them to Jesus."

Shaking off the numbness, I tell myself to get it together.

"Tell your father that Jesus wants to go to the Garden of Gethsemane after the Passover supper. So tonight makes the most sense to execute the plan."

Immediately, my mind goes to the discussion with Peter. That's the place Jesus goes to spend time in prayer.

"It will be dark with little to no one around to cause a scene. Plus, the chief priests have no more patience. They want it done now."

Judas punches the palm of his hand with his fist.

"Seth, remind your father I will go up to Jesus and kiss him on his cheek to identify to the guards he is the one to arrest. Tell Aran to be calm and wait for my cue. We don't need your father to mess things up if he overreacts. Now go."

Off I go. It's getting real now. On my walk to the Sheep Gate to meet up with Father, I think back to the day we started following Jesus. Tonight will be it. Once the guards arrest Jesus, it will be all over for me and Father. We will have done our part. We can return to our more normal life of crime. Matter of fact, Father has said by helping the chief priest and the high government officials, we will be set for life. Not sure if they told Father that or if he is hoping for it. If so, I might become a chief tax collector. Who knows?

As I approach the Sheep Gate, I see a group of men huddled together, gambling and rolling dice against the wall. They are using language that is dirtier than they are. Right in the middle of the filth stands Father, who is about to throw the dice.

"Father," I say, "I need to talk to you."

He looks over his shoulder at me with disgust. He is not delighted to see me. "Boy," he argues, "can't you see I'm about to take the last bit of money these poor slobs have to lose? It had better be important."

"I have a message from Judas."

Father drops the dice, and without looking to see what his fate is, he walks over to me and pulls me aside. "What's the message?"

"Tonight is the night to arrest Jesus."

"What? Judas wants Jesus arrested tonight?"

I nod. "You and I are to tell the chief priests that Jesus will be in the Garden of Gethsemane later tonight. That will be a great time and place because there won't be large crowds. Jesus won't have a lot of his people with him. His arrest should be quick and easy."

Father reaches his arms up and places them firmly on my shoulders.

"This is so exciting. I've been waiting for this moment for a long time."

"Judas wanted me to remind you to stay with the plan. The plan is Judas will go up to Jesus and kiss him on his cheek so the guards can identify Jesus and arrest him."

Father seems agitated. He answers, "Sure, I won't mess it up. I know what the plan is. I'm no dummy like you are."

Father never misses an opportunity to bring me down a notch or two. Maybe I should go up to Father and kiss him on his cheek so the guards will arrest him instead of Jesus.

"Father, I know you know what the plan is. I'm just saying what Judas told me to."

Without saying another word, he takes off toward the royal court. I follow, making sure to keep a step behind him. We get around to the porch that leads up to the temple mount. For Father to climb the towering marble steps takes every breath he has to reach the giant doors at the top. As we near them, two guards greet us.

Father motions for me to stop as he approaches one of the men. The guard never makes eye contact with him. Father tells the guard something. The guard turns and enters the temple. Father turns and heads back to me.

"Okay, Seth, it's done. Tonight, Jesus will be stopped for good from speaking lies against the teachings of the temple. We are just hours away from being part of history. It's my wish that you and I will be talked about for generations to come."

Father takes off down the royal porch, and I follow. As we head toward the Garden of Gethsemane, my mind goes to Tabitha. How would she feel about me if she found out my part in this? I think of her often. I still love her so much. What will our lives be like when this is all over? Will I ever see her again?

Chapter Thirty-Eight

Seth

This is a first for me. I have never seen the Garden of Gethsemane. Even at night under the light of the moon, I can see why Jesus likes this place. It's beautiful. White lilies are planted around the base of olive trees that form a lovely canopy.

Mother would love to see all these white flowers brightening the backdrop of the dark sky. When I was a kid, I would come home from a swim at the pond. Along the way, I would pick flowers for her and she would gush over them for days. Mother always had flowers in the house. Father, of course, would complain that they made the house smell bad and that they were too girly.

If my father thinks the garden is beautiful tonight, he says nothing. He's all business. "Seth," he says, "find a place to hide and keep an eye out for Jesus. I'll head back up the path to meet the guards to bring them to Judas and Jesus."

"Sure thing, Father, I think I can handle that."

I leave the conversational door wide open for Father to say something mean back to me, but to my surprise, there's only silence, not a word. I hear nothing except footsteps heading down the path.

I'm not sure how long I was there or how long I was asleep against a tree, but voices woke me. Thankfully, because I was dreaming I took Tabitha a vase full of white lilies with crimson red sprinkled on all the petals. I told her I was sorry for not believing her, that I knew she was a changed woman since that day at the well with Jesus. Tabitha told me she forgave me. She was grateful I accepted and believed how her life had changed, full of the living water of life from Jesus—forgiveness and grace. I kept telling her that I didn't deserve forgiveness. Rattling off all the bad things I had done. The list was long and didn't exclude many things that would be considered bad or sinful. I could check off most of the Ten Commandments as being broken. And if I live long enough, I might hit them all. I could never do enough to ever deserve forgiveness. I was beyond enough.

With tears filling her eyes, she told me that no one lives a life deserving of salvation, God's forgiveness. "Yes, you are right," she said. "You can never do enough *enoughs.* That's the reason Jesus was sent to be with us for this short time. Forgiveness is a gift wrapped in the arms of His son, Jesus. A gift of grace, of unconditional love for you."

I'm not sure what that dream meant, but I know I care deeply for Tabitha, and I think she probably cares more for me than I ever thought she did. I can't explain this feeling, but I believe no matter what happens, she will always be there for me.

Peeking around the olive trees, I see Jesus, Peter, and two other disciples standing about twenty feet away from me. I quietly crawl down the row of olive trees to get close enough to hear what they are saying. I plant my hand on a small twig filled with tiny, sharp thorns. It takes everything I have in me to not scream out from the pain running through the palm of my hand. I stop and start picking thorn after thorn out of my skin.

That moment takes me back to when I was a little boy playing by some rosebushes down the path from our house. I fell into one, and dozens of thorns pierced me all over my body. I ran home as fast as I could, holding my arms stretched out by my sides, crying out to Father to remove them, to take away the pain. Father simply turned his back and walked away.

Jesus' voice calls me back to the present. "Peter," he says, "you, James, and John sit here. I am going over to that stone."

He points to a boulder about twenty feet away. Jesus looks troubled about something. He's weary to the point of sorrow, a deep sadness. I have never seen him look this way. Jesus then tells them, "I have never felt this grief before. It's almost to the point of death. Stay here and keep watch for me."

Jesus turns and walks over to the stone. Dropping to his knees, then lying fully on the ground, he speaks as if there is someone right next to him.

"My Father, Abba! If you are willing, remove this cup from me if there is any other way; yet not my will, but yours be done."

After lying on the ground for about an hour, Jesus stands and walks over to Peter, James, and John.

He kicks each one with his sandal as they lie asleep, slumped over one another. With disappointment, he says, "Hey! Wake up. Can't you three stay awake for even an hour? I would like for you guys to keep watch for me."

All three straighten up and begin fumbling for words, "Oh no, I wasn't asleep, I'm awake for you, Jesus."

Peter makes the bold statement. "I would never go to sleep if you asked me not to."

Jesus looks at them and says, "Let's try it again, guys. Please stay awake this time."

He returns to the stone and says what he said the first time, but with more intensity. Another hour passes, and for a second time, Jesus returns to find his so-called watchers fast asleep. For a third time, Jesus returns to his well-established spot on the ground in front of the stone.

"Abba Father," he prays, "is there any other way? If not,

your will be done, not mine."

This time his pleading is the most powerful one that I've heard. He is now sweating profusely. Then I see his drops of sweat, which are running down his forehead, turn to blood red. I have never seen anyone sweat drops of blood before tonight.

After another hour, Jesus stands, wipes the blood sweat from his face, and walks toward his disciples.

"Okay, guys," he says, "you can wake up now. I'm done. The time for the one who is going to betray me is near."

As Peter, James, and John wake up, wiping the sleep from their eyes and struggling to get up from their naps, Judas leads a small group of high priests, temple elders, and guards. Father is bringing up the rear. Many, including Father, are carrying swords and clubs as they approach Jesus.

Yes, the beginning of the end is near.

Chapter Thirty-Nine

Judas doesn't miss a beat. He walks right up to Jesus and says, "Rabbi." Then he kisses Jesus on his left cheek.

Jesus says, "Judas, are you betraying the Son of man with a kiss?"

Peter steps forward and pulls a sword out from under his robe. He swings it toward one man standing next to one of the high priests. In one swift motion, Peter cuts off the man's right ear.

I gag at seeing this, almost losing what little I had eaten in the last few hours.

"Peter!" Jesus shouts. "What are doing? Stop! No more of this."

Jesus reaches down and picks up the man's ear and presses it in place, restoring it, healing it. The man's ear is right back in its place and looks as if it was never harmed.

"Peter, the scriptures must be fulfilled this way," Jesus says.

Like a roaring lion, Jesus then turns toward the group of men who are there to seize him. "Look at all of you carrying swords and clubs coming after me as if I'm going to put up some kind of fight and endanger your lives. If that were my plan, why wouldn't I have done that before? For days I have sat in the temple teaching, and you did not take me. No, all this must happen as the scriptures of the prophets have said it would."

One of the high priests raises his arm high to the sky and yells, "Seize him! Take him now! Take him to Annas first!"

Four Roman guards run to Jesus and shackle his wrists. As they take charge of him, Peter, James, and John sneak away.

I come out from behind the tree and walk over to Father. He is pounding the club against the ground as if he had just conquered the tallest of giants all by himself. He looks at me and says, "We did it. We are heroes forever. The high officials will call out our names from this day on, showering us with praise and honor. Our reward is yet to come."

I think about it, too. It is over. My boyhood friend has been arrested. Maybe this will now allow me to have the relationship with my father I've always wanted. Maybe he will say to me, "I am proud of you." But is this betrayal what I want my father to praise me for? I shake myself back into reality and realize what is done is done.

Jesus shows no sign of any resistance, and so the six guards—two on either side plus one a step in front and one a step behind—lead Jesus away. They follow behind the high priests. Then come the temple elders. My father trails behind.

It's just a short walk back into the city, and we end up at a large building connected to the temple. We walk up ten marble steps that lead toward two tall, carved wood doors. A stooped, elderly man greets us, and he gestures for us to follow him.

As I enter the building, I can see it has another floor above us, and there is a dark hall leading to what appears to be a lower level.

We follow the guards, who guide Jesus into a large, round chamber room. Purple curtains hang opposite the entrance. Hundreds of candles in sconces light the room. A crowd of at least a hundred priests, high priests, and elders of the council are waiting there.

So this is the Sanhedrin, an assembly of the elders

appointed to sit as a tribunal. It is a court for the Jews. The men serve as the supreme religious body of the Jewish people.

As Jesus gets closer to them, a chorus of mumbling disdain grows louder and louder, revealing a deep disrespect and hatred. It reminds me of stories I heard about the Colosseum and the spectators chanting for the defeat of the gladiators or the murder of an innocent civilian thrown into the ring with bloodthirsty lions.

I sense the men in charge are here for blood. A wave of anger swells from the crowd I have not felt before. As I look at face after face of those waiting for Jesus to enter the ring, the hair on my arms stands straight up, and a chill runs down my back. My body twitches uncontrollably.

The guards position Jesus in the center of the room. A hush comes over the room, and the purple curtains part as a man enters. A man of lower rank follows him. The first man wears a beautiful robe decorated with colorful stones that sparkle as the candlelight bounces off them. He sits down in a chair that is big enough for five.

His assistant raises a hand to the crowd. "Good evening," he says, "I am Annas, the father-in-law of High Priest, Caiaphas. Is this man you bring here tonight the one who calls himself Jesus?"

The crowd erupts in angry shouts. An elder motions them to be quiet and then says, "This is Jesus, the one who claims he is the way, and the truth, and the life. He claims no one comes to his father but through him."

Annas turns away from the crowd and gestures for Caiaphas to take over.

The high priest studies Jesus for a moment then looks around the room. "What evidence do you have to prove this man, Jesus, is guilty of any wrongdoing and worthy of the death sentence?"

Death sentence? How did we get from throwing Jesus in prison to "Let's kill him"? Is Tabitha right? Have they wanted to kill Jesus all along?

I walk over to Father. "I thought the officials wanted to put Jesus in prison. I thought they just wanted to shut him up. You never said anything about killing him."

Father smirks. "Seth, you naive boy. Yes, they want to stop Jesus from spreading his so-called Good News forever. Putting him to death will do that. And you and I will be heroes for it."

Tabitha is right. They want to kill Jesus, and Father was a part of the plan all along. I guess I am also guilty of believing a man who would beat a child.

Caiaphas listens to the chief priests and elders of the council who do their best to come up with solid proof to justify Jesus' death sentence, but nothing sticks. After each person tells his story to convict Jesus, Jesus stands there, silent.

Father and I had been hired to spy on Jesus, and we had gathered information that seemed to be what they were looking for. Father steps out of the crowd and says to the high priest, "High Priest Caiaphas, my son and I have followed Jesus during his preaching travels, and I can tell you that he claimed he can destroy the temple and rebuild it in three days."

Caiaphas jumps up and shouts to Jesus, "Man! Why do you not answer what all these people say against you? I urge you, beg you, to tell us whether you are the Christ, the Son of God."

Jesus keeps his head bent. His shackled hands are folded together in front of him. Suddenly he looks up. Scanning the crowd, left to right, then looking straight ahead, he says confidently, "I am, and you shall see the Son of man sitting at the right hand of power, and coming with the clouds of heaven."

Caiaphas tears his magnificent robe from neck to ankle and shouts in a rage, "This man has spoken sacrilegiously about God! Isn't this disrespectful talk enough to warrant his death for the crime of blasphemy? Now what do you think about this man Jesus?"

The room erupts with chants. "Death! He deserves to die! Death to him!"

Then, out of nowhere, with Father joining in, they spit in Jesus' face and punch him. And all the time Jesus takes it. There is nothing he can do. There is no one to rescue him. Not one of his disciples is in sight. Caiaphas stands with his torn robe lying on the floor at his feet. He yells to the angry mob, "Get him out of here! Take this blasphemer away from me. Take him to Pilate. The governor will surely deliver the sentence of death Jesus deserves."

The high priest, wearing only his linen underclothing, steps over his robe. Guards immediately escort him out of the room. The guards push back the crowd and quickly escort Jesus. As the guards pull Jesus away, he and I exchange glances. I wonder how many more times I will see Jesus alive.

Chapter Forty

The dark hall of the tribunal chamber leading downstairs is, in fact, the way to a dungeon. Interesting place. You can go from saying a prayer to becoming a prisoner without ever having to leave the building. It is too late to travel to see Governor Pilate, so this is where the guards will keep Jesus the rest of the night.

This is not a place I would want to spend many nights. At least five tall iron doors are separated by thick stone walls. The walls stretch from the muddy floor up to the ten-foot ceiling. A small slit in the rock wall pretends to be a window. It isn't doing much good. It is dark and smelly. I have been around some bad-smelling places, and this is the worst. I'm doing everything I can to breathe out my mouth and not my nose.

I'm not sure which cell Jesus ended up in. I can't see through the group of guards, and the dismal lighting doesn't help either. I manage to find a dark corner in which to lie low while Jesus waits for his next inquisition.

My hiding spot is warmer and smells better, at least that's what I am telling myself.

Right at the time I'm about to drift off to sleep, a guard shouts, "Get up! It's time to go!" He rattles the iron door, making sure whoever is in there is awake along with everybody else. The echo of the rattling goes on for what seems forever. All the guards stand in attention and take their places as they walk past me in the dark hall. Jesus is in the middle of the procession; I fall in behind them. My guess is they are taking Jesus to Governor Pilate as Caiaphas directed them to do last night.

It doesn't matter. I'm going to follow anyway.

The guards head west when we get outside. It's still dark, perhaps an hour or so till sunrise.

As we approach the palace, the crowds are already gathered. It is a struggle to get through. More guards join in to push back the people. No way are all these people going to get into the palace. Outside in the upper city, there are grand courtyards with beautifully sculpted trees and bushes. Fountains are sprinkled throughout the foliage, providing for wildlife and emitting hypnotic sounds.

The guards begin directing the crowd to wait in the courtyard. The walking paths fill, spilling people into the gardens. Many carry large walking sticks. I keep in step with the guards, staying close behind.

This is the former palace of Herod the Tetrarch. From stories I have heard, inside the hall, magnificent artwork in gold frames covers the impressively high walls. Silver and gold vases are spread throughout the large reception room. I would love to see it myself someday. Everyone in Jerusalem knows that Pilate and his wife stay here when they are in the city.

I find it interesting that none of his disciples are here except the one who started all this with a kiss on the cheek—Judas. But he looks troubled, not victorious. Is that regret I see on his face? He goes up to the group of chief priests and elders. I creep closer.

"I've changed my mind," Judas says. His voice is high-pitched with anxiety. "I don't want the thirty pieces of silver you paid me for giving Jesus over to you. I have done wrong by betraying him. He is an innocent man."

His confession surprises me. Has he truly repented for his actions? He didn't say Jesus was who he said he was. No, he said only that he was an innocent man.

Four guards lift their trumpet horns and let out a blast to announce the entrance of Governor Pilate. Pilate walks out to the edge of a raised marble platform. He looks down at the mass of people gathered and says, "Guards, bring your accused closer to me."

The guards walk Jesus forward and position him just under the platform. Pilate looks down at Jesus from his judgment seat and says, "I have one simple question for you. Are you the king of the Jews?"

Jesus looks up at Pilate. "It is as you say."

The crowd goes wild, shouting, "He is a blasphemer!"

"He is a liar!"

"He is no king of the Jews!"

"He calls himself the Christ, no way!"

Insult after insult is hurled at Jesus, accusing him of being everything except who he says he is.

Raising his hand, Pilate quiets the crowd and asks Jesus, "Don't you hear all the things they accuse you of? Yet you just stand there not saying a word, not defending yourself."

Pilate now throws up both his hands. "Then what shall I do with this man Jesus, who is called Christ, King of the Jews?"

One by one, those carrying walking sticks pound them on the paths of the courtyard. The noise echoes through the area louder and louder. Then the people in the crowd chant in unison, "Crucify him . . . Crucify him . . . Crucify him!"

The noise is so loud I have to cover my ears. A voice I can recognize anywhere is Father's. He's yelling as loud as he can, "Crucify him!"

Pilate motions for one of his servants to bring him a basin. He places both hands deep inside.

"People, you bring before me a man who has been questioned by Annas and the High Priest Caiaphas. I have received word from Herod himself that he wants nothing to do with Jesus. You demand that he be punished, put to death.

So, let it be."

The crowd erupts, proclaiming victory.

Rubbing his hands as he removes them from the water basin, he looks around at all the people. They settle to a quiet hush when Pilate holds up his wet hands, the water now dripping down his head.

"See, I wash my hands. I want you all to see I am innocent of this man's blood."

Pilate gestures to the guards to take Jesus away. Jesus' fate has been set. The wishes of the priests, the elders, and the haters like my father have been granted. Pilate gives the people what they want—Jesus' blood.

I can't say I feel remorse, but a tear falls to my cheek as the guards lead Jesus out. The people in the courtyard spit at him and mock "the king," all the while continuing to shout, "Crucify him!"

Chapter Forty-One

As the guards escort Jesus out of the palace's grand hall, someone comes up on my right and another someone comes up on my left. Both of my forearms are suddenly squeezed tight enough to cause discomfort. Before I can protest, the guard on my right says, "We are to take you to the chief priest and the governor."

They whisk me away with no further explanation. I am not sure if this has to do with the reward for the work Father I have done or not. It doesn't seem like a reward-getting escort. They force me to walk at a fast pace, and I feel more like a captive. Two more guards approach from my left. They are handling Father in the same rough manner. His lips are moving nonstop, yet there's no sign anything he says is being heard or even matters.

The guards take us back behind a curtain that separates the grand hall from other parts of the palace. We pass at least ten rooms before the guards turn into one that is dark and unimpressive. The small room has one little window and a wood table piled high with parchments. Seven chairs are placed around the long, rectangular table. One chair is at the head and three flank each side. The guards stop us at the end of the table that doesn't have a chair. A door I hadn't noticed opens inward, and Pilate enters the room followed by six chief priests. They don't say a word as they take their places at the table. Father and I look at each other. He shrugs his shoulder as to say, "I don't know what's going on."

The priest seated at the right of the governor looks up at us. "Gentlemen," he says, "we have brought you here to inform you what is to happen next. As you know, because of the work both of you have done, and the other evidence gathered, we have just sentenced Jesus to be crucified. Lying here in front of us on the table are, as you can see, records of all that have been gathered and turned in to help convict Jesus to his death. His lies, false teachings, and his profession to being the Christ all end in a couple of days. But that's not all. We have found you to be long-time thieves, stealing from the innocent for years. We know, Aran, that you have not just caused financial harm to many, but you have hurt people who did not play by your rules. You are a bad man, and you have trained your son to be just like you. We also know, Aran, that you and your son, Seth, were responsible for the temple robbery some years ago."

Father speaks out. "Some years ago, that was almost twenty years ago! How can you hold that against us now?"

"We couldn't until we had solid evidence, and you just admitted it to all of us, including the governor."

Father drops his head, realizing he told them what they needed to convict us.

"Aran, you and your son must also pay for your wrongdoings, for the crimes that you have committed. We sentence both of you to death, alongside Jesus."

It takes a second for those three words to sink in. *Sentenced. To. Death.*

Father, whose head is still bent, has tears rolling off his cheeks. I am too shocked to say anything or to express any emotions. I stand there with a frozen gaze, looking at Father cry like a baby.

A voice breaks the silence. "Do either of you have anything you would like to say before the guards take you away?"

I turn my head to the voice at the table and say,

"Governor, my father and I thought all along that we were helping in this cause to arrest Jesus so he would stop spreading his false teachings, as you see them. Your goal was to have the temple priests' teachings seen as the only truth. I thought we were to help only in Jesus's arrest, not his death sentence."

The men sitting around the table laughed. One of them says, "Don't be so naive. Your father knew all along what the plans for Jesus were. Rotting in a prison wasn't one of them."

I continue. "You want to kill Jesus because you're afraid of him. What if he's right? You're right about two things: I am guilty of my crimes and Father is guilty of his crimes. You'd better be right in saying Jesus is guilty. If not, for your sakes, I hope the opportunity to receive grace and forgiveness he talked about over these past years is true."

The governor shouts, "Guards, take them away!"

Without hesitation, the guards snap to attention and take hold of us. They escort us down the hall. Many people are still standing in the halls talking about the death sentence given to Jesus just minutes before. They aren't there shouting praises to me and Father for what we did to ensure the arrest. No, they couldn't care less about us. Some even shouted, "Hang them too!"

To my surprise, Tabitha is standing with several others. All are crying, distraught from the proclamation of Jesus' soon-to-be crucifixion. I stop, forcing the guards to stop suddenly. They squeeze my arm even harder. I plead with them. "Please, stop! Please let me have a word with my friend, that woman, for just a moment."

I point to Tabitha. One guard grumbles, "Make it quick, and don't try to get away. It won't be good for you or your friend."

The guards escorting Father walk on.

I walk toward Tabitha with the two oversized guards matching my every step.

"Tabitha . . ."

She can tell something is very wrong. She looks straight into my eyes, ignoring the towering muscle-bound guard by my side, while taking my hands in hers.

"Seth, why are the guards holding you? Are you being arrested?"

I nod. How I wish the guards weren't there so I could hold her one last time. "They are going to put me and Father on a cross right next to Jesus. We have been convicted of all our crimes. I'm not too surprised. I thought it might catch up with me someday. Well, today is the day."

Tabitha breaks down in tears, reaching to put her arms around me. But the guards step in to block her. As one pulls me back, the other brute steps between us. "No touching," he says. "Hurry. We have to go."

"Tabitha, will you please let my mother know what happened? Please tell her how much I love her. Tell her no matter what happens to me, I will always have her in my heart. Please watch after her if you can."

With that, the guards pull me away, and off we go. I look back, and Tabitha nods—yes, she'll do it. The guards push me through a large iron door, and we walk down several levels of spiraling stone steps until we end up in the deep recesses of the palace. It is dark except for several small candles burning in sconces mounted on the stone walls. It is cold. The smell in the air is thick with a mixture of wet hay, spoiled meat, and human body waste.

The guards lead me past a cell from which emanates Father cursing. He's blaming the priests, council members, many others, and, of course, Jesus for his predicament. He's ranting and raving that it's never his fault.

In his world, people blame someone else for the woes of their lives.

In reality, most of our woes result from the wrong choices we make. I can raise my hand to that. I could sit in my cell and cry and bemoan that Father was a big reason for my troubles, but it's not all true. I had a choice. I did what I did, right or wrong.

As I try to get settled in my cold, drafty, stink-filled four-by-six stone box, a voice speaks softly through a small iron grate in the stone wall. "Seth, do you know who I am?"

"Jesus, is that you?"

"Yes. I would say I am sorry you are here too, but maybe this is the best place for you to be. Perhaps this cold, smelly cell in the pit of the darkness with a rat or two crawling at your feet will get your attention now. There is and always has been something better for your life. Grace. God's grace. You can truly shine with the warm, sweet smell of grace that will release you, give you life."

"Jesus, my fate has been set. How is God's grace going to help me now? It is too late for me. There is no chance of release for me."

"Seth, don't you still have breath in you?"

"Yes."

"Then it's never too late. As long as you have breath, you can say yes."

"Jesus, I'm glad I can talk to you, even though I can't see you. I know you are there listening to me."

"Seth, that's the same with the heavenly Father. I can talk to him anytime, anywhere, without ever seeing him. I know he is there, hearing my every word."

My father interrupts us. "Would you two please shut up? All that talk about last breath and talking to some unseen god. You two are crazy. Seth, you should know by now that everything Jesus says is a lie. The main reason we are here is because of him. We are going to be nailed to two splintery wood planks because of him. You should hate him for that."

There's a pause while Father catches his breath, readying for round two. "Hey, Jesus," he says, "if you say you are this great king, why don't you just call on your heavenly Father to set you free?"

I move to the door. "Father, be quiet. You are here

because of all the crimes and wrong things you have committed. Be a man for once and own up to that."

"Seth, that a boy! For once you are acting like a real man and telling me what you think. Is it because there are three feet of stone wall separating us? The only thing I'm guilty of is living a life I wanted to live. And I will live my life that way until I take my last breath."

There's another pause. Then Jesus speaks kindly. "Aran, Seth, I tell you this: it's never too late for either of you until your last breath is expelled from your mouth. For generations to come, many will say yes to the grace offered. Unfortunately, too many will not. One day my birth will be celebrated, my death will be memorialized, and the true understanding of the rebuilding of the temple in three days will be debated. And this I know for sure, my sadness for those who don't accept me as their Lord and Savior will tear at my heart more than any beatings or nails piercing my body ever could. The only choice I can make for you will come soon on a cross. The choice to believe is not mine to make. Every person will have to answer that themselves."

All three cells become silent. Then I hear what sounds like someone softly crying and talking. I walk over to my cell door and look through a small crack between the door and the stone wall. A guard is kneeling at the door of Jesus' cell.

Chapter Forty-Two

"Jesus, are you awake?"

"Yes, Seth, I am. What do you need?"

I walk over to get closer to the metal grate in between our cells.

"Well, for the past few hours I've listened to Father rant about how innocent he is and call you every bad name under the sun. I have been thinking about what you said to us right after the guards threw us in this dungeon."

"Okay, what's on your mind?"

"You said you would be saddened by those who don't accept you, that it would be worse for you than any other pain you could experience. Why? Why do you care so much for those who don't care for you?" I slap the solid rock wall separating our cells knowing he's not going to hear my frustration. How can someone be so forgiving?

"You know many people like my father who hate you. Why do you care for those who simply ignore you? They may not hate you, but they just don't believe what you have to say. I don't hate you, Jesus, but I'm not a believer. I'm not one of your followers."

"I know, and that breaks my heart. Let me explain it this way. Imagine if a man has a hundred sheep and one wanders away, and he has no idea where it went. Being a good shepherd of his flock, he will leave the ninety-nine to go look for it. He desperately wants to find it, to save the one that is lost. Now, if the man finds it, truly I say to you, he will rejoice over it more than the ninety-nine that have not wandered off. So, it is not the will of your Father who is in heaven that one, even one, should be lost."

An exasperated Father speaks up. "You guys counting sheep is making me sleepy. Jesus, do you have other wild tails to tell us? I would like to go to sleep so I don't have to listen to the drivel from the two of you."

"Father, shut up! Maybe you should listen to what Jesus has to say for once."

My cell door begins to vibrate. The sound of metal scratching metal pierces my ears to the point they hurt. It sounds as if my cell could come crumbling down on top of me. The grate in the rock wall shakes. I take a step back, hoping fate won't leave me here buried under the stones.

An angry shout comes from the hallway. "Prisoners! Shut up. No more talking."

"Thanks, guard!" Father shouts back. "One last thing. Hey Jesus, have you heard about your friend Judas? Word from one guard is that he can be seen swinging from a tree. That's one of your lost sheep who's never coming back."

Laughter trickles down my way. Father's laugh is spiteful. Always has been.

"Aran, your life is a lot like Judas's—a sad one. You both have spent a lot of time with me, watching me perform miracle after miracle. With your own eyes, you've witnessed the blind regain their sight, the lepers cleansed, and the lame walking. Judas and your son saw me walk on water in the deepest part of the lake. I came away as dry as a bone. I fed thousands, more than once, with nothing more than scraps. You filled your stomach with the blessing of the Lord. Yet you desire what is of the world and not what the heavenly Father offers. There will be many generations to come that will say yes to me and believe I am who I say I am. They will believe by faith alone. Aran, you saw and even took part in my ministry, yet you are blind."

The large metal door at the end of the row of cells rattles open. A stern voice yells down the corridor, "It is time."

I know what that means. It is time for our days on earth to end. Maybe the stone walls falling on me would have been more merciful.

The clatter of the guards' swords bouncing off their shields as they walk toward our cells grows louder and louder as they approach. What they plan for us should never happen to anyone. My mind goes back to when I was a young boy being marched by my father to the side of the barn. The beatings flooded my mind, making my body twitch with pain just from the thought.

The guards walk us outside into a large courtyard. Jesus is led out in front of Father and me. The Centurion, who is standing before us, raises his hands in the air, which encourages all the guards to shout vile words and mock Jesus as he passes. They don't stop at just hurling words at him. One by one, they throw their fists in Jesus' face.

Each punch causes Jesus' knees to buckle, and the guards hold him up, making sure the next guard has a solid target to hit. His head is being pummeled like no other beating I have seen before, and I have seen a lot of fights. They were common and brutal, but this is the worst. With every punch, a new bruise is added to Jesus' face. His skin turns all kinds of colors: black, and blue, with red flowing from his nose and lips. I wondered if he would even survive the beatings to be alive for what comes next. As I walk through the group of soldiers, I wait anxiously for the fists to rain down on me. To my surprise, they don't. Nothing happens to me or Father. The beatings and verbal abuse are just for Jesus.

The guards have to hold him up to make sure he can stand upright in front of the centurion who yells, "Strip him of his clothes!"

Two guards approach Jesus, and without hesitation, rip off his clothes. The centurion throws a robe at Jesus. "King of the Jews, here's your robe. Put it on—now! Every king should wear a beautiful purple robe. Oh, and you need a staff."

He throws a long, crooked stick at him.

"Anything else I'm forgetting?"

One guard mocks, "How about a crown? Where's his crown?"

"Yes!" the centurion proclaims. "A king needs a crown. Where do we get a crown fit for the King of the Jews?" He looks off to the side and says, "I know, we will make him a crown with the branches from that jujube tree. Cut off its branches, and we will use them for the king's crown."

Three dutiful soldiers respond. They run toward the shrub and begin cutting branches filled with thorns. The little spikes grow in pairs on either side of the branches. They then twist the branches together, making a circle with thorn after thorn standing at attention.

While the crown of thorns is being made, the guards mock Jesus again, spitting in his face, throwing more punches at him, kicking him. They make sure that not any part of his body is ignored. As blood flows from his body, grimy spit mingles in.

Just as I think it can't get any worse, the guards hand the crown to the centurion, who says, "Attention everyone, quiet. I now hold in my hand the crown made just for the King of Jews. It is time he receives his crown."

The guards hold up Jesus by supporting him under his armpits, presenting him before the centurion. With his hands stretched out in front of him as if he were going to offer Jesus a welcome embrace, the centurion mocks. "Jesus, I present you with this crown."

The roar grows as the crowd swells beyond the soldiers to thousands of people wanting to ridicule Jesus. The sound is deafening.

The centurion takes the crown with its jagged thorns and places it firmly on top of Jesus' head. That would have been enough for me, but then the centurion pulls out his sword from its sheath. Holding his sword flat, he raises it over Jesus' head and says, "Jesus, I . . . CROWN . . . YOU . . . KING . . . OF . . . THE . . . JEWS!"

With each word, he slams his sword down on top of the crown, making sure every thorn sinks deeper and deeper into Jesus' skull.

It takes all the strength the two guards have to hold Jesus up under the barrage of hits. With every hit of the sword, the people cheer louder and louder.

I look away, but Father, who is standing next to me, laughs. He's encouraging the guards. "Do it again. Harder this time." He joins in with the mocking, saying "Hail thee! Hail thee, King of the Jews!"

The bystanders kneel and bow as they mock him.

I wonder when will enough be enough?

Chapter Forty-Three

Seth

"Your King of Jews is ready now," the general says. "Take him and the other two to Golgotha."

The general turns Jesus around as if to present him to the people. As they lead us away, I can see Jesus can't walk without the help from the guards. He's struggling, but he seems determined to do it. I'm struggling too. I never thought they wanted to put Jesus through all this abuse. Even though I don't agree with his teachings, I'm not sure he deserves all this. Father, however, doesn't miss a beat hurling insults and spitting at Jesus, even though he's too far away for his spittle to land on him.

Golgotha, also known as The Skull, is located just outside the city walls on a busy road. Our crucifixions will be exhibited there for the very purpose of letting people— both the good and the bad—see what happens if they don't play by their rules, the rules of the Romans. Even though Father and I had seen bodies on exhibit there, we never thought someday we would hang on a cross alongside the road in Golgotha.

Along the walk, more and more people gather to say insulting things to Jesus and mock him. As we get closer to Golgotha, greater numbers of people weep and seem deeply saddened for Jesus. I think I might have even spotted some of his disciples in the crowd. It's hard to tell. The crowd looks like one big mass of bodies.

This I know for sure: no one is here to shed a tear for me or Father. Then suddenly, my mind goes to Tabitha. I wonder if she is here? Not here for me, but maybe for Jesus?

As the guards escort us to the top of the hill, I see three crosses lying flat on the ground. They take Jesus first. They strip him down to his loincloth. The guards grab his robe as if it is some kind of souvenir to be sold off to the highest bidder.

The guards lay Jesus down on top of the cross. One guard stretches Jesus' left arm straight out from his side, turning his palm up. Another guard takes Jesus' right arm and does the same. Now that he's in position, the third guard reaches into a wooden box. I can hear metal on metal clinking together as he searches for the right one. Having found a suitable nail, he places the long metal spike in the center of Jesus' hand and, with a large, wood mallet, rains down swing after swing, driving the nail into Jesus' hand. The nail tears the skin away before cracking through his bones. This same terrifying scene happens again to the other hand. It is too much for me to take. I feel a sickness in my stomach like no other. I also know my turn is coming. My life will be over soon.

As Jesus lies there, he never says a word. His breathing slows as his chest rises gently and then falls. He knows what is next. The guard takes Jesus' feet and places them one on top of the other. Then he reaches for a longer nail and places its tip on the top of Jesus' feet. Again the mallet swings down with greater force, and the nail tears through the top foot but doesn't move from there. After four or five ferocious swings at the nail, the guard becomes frustrated. He pulls out the nail from the top of Jesus' foot, places his feet side-by-side, and starts all over again. This time, he drives a nail into each foot.

I can only imagine how painful that must have been for Jesus. But soon I won't have to imagine. It's about to happen to me.

Now that Jesus is nailed to the cross, several other guards step up, and with one synchronized movement, lift the cross. As the movement jolts him around, Jesus groans in pain. With no warning, the guards step forward and drop the cross into a hole in the ground. The cross sinks at least three feet before it stops abruptly.

Jesus winces from the jarring and tearing of his body, but he still says nothing.

The guards approach Father and me to repeat the same hideous task of nailing us to the crosses. But one guard walks over to where Jesus is hanging, and he leans a wooden ladder up against the back of the cross. With one hand, he holds on to the ladder as he steps higher and higher. In his other hand is a piece of wood. Reaching the top of the ladder, the guard turns the piece of wood around and takes a nail and hammer from his belt. He nails the wood at the top of the cross right above Jesus' head. It reads: THIS IS JESUS, THE KING OF THE JEWS.

Chapter Forty-Four

Bang . . .
  Bang . . .
  Bang.
As the wooden mallet pounds the dull, rusty nail into my hand, the pain is more than I can take. Oh, please let that be the last one. Father's beatings feel like a mere slap on the wrist compared to a nail plunging through my bone. Just breathe. It will be over soon.
  Bang . . .
  Bang . . .
  Bang.
Please let it stop! The blood snakes down my arms and legs. The sweat runs down my head and into my eyes, but I can still see well enough to watch as the guard pulls out what I hope is the final nail. I lie here, taking nail after nail into my body in silence. Not ten feet from me, my father screams and cries with every nail that is pounded into his body.

The guards treat me the same way they did Jesus; they leave me upright before plunging the cross into the ground. They lift the wood beams, take a step forward, and then drop me in a never-ending hole. Knowing the stop is coming, I try to prepare myself for the pain. Too late. The jolt feels as if every nerve in my body is being pulled out as each nail tears my flesh. I scream like I never have before.

As I work desperately to catch my breath, hundreds of

people gather at the base of the hill to watch us suffer. A few people have moved closer. A woman is on her knees in front of me and another kneels at the feet of Jesus. Between them is a third woman. Her arms are draped over each of their shoulders. The woman in the middle looks up. Tears flow from her eyes as she mouths the words, "I love you."

Tabitha! It's Tabitha. She is here. I want to climb down off this cross and take her in my arms. But reality sets in. That isn't going to happen. Nothing good will ever happen again.

The other two women look up. It's Mother. And Mary.

They are here for us—their sons. It breaks my heart that Mother has to see me for the last time hanging on a cross. I'm sure Jesus feels the same. Neither of them deserves this.

Each little move I make is an intense reminder of the nails that tore through me. Every breath now is slow and painful. With every ounce of life I have in me I straighten up to look at Mother. With all the strength I have left, I say softly, "I am so sorry . . . I love you." I look at Tabitha and say, "Please take care of her for me . . . I will always love you."

They nod. Amid all of my pain, I feel a moment of relief knowing they heard.

That special moment with Mother and Tabitha comes to a quick end when the crowd begins to hurl insults at Jesus again. The crowd grows louder and angrier.

One man shouts at Jesus, "Hey! You who are going to destroy the temple and rebuild it in three days, save yourself, and come down from the cross!"

Other voices scream, "Just come down off that cross, perform one of your miracles," and "Let this Christ, the king of Israel, now come down from the cross, so that we may see and believe!"

On and on it goes. Then I hear my father's cackling voice say, "Yes, Jesus, why don't you save yourself? You always wanted us to think you are someone special, but you are no more than a weak man. You're no king. Not my king."

Father says all he can considering the intense pain. He has a marked slowness of breath as he yells out as loud as his body will let him, "Hey, everybody, look, I Aran . . . am being crucified next to the want-to-be king, Jesus." He trails off into pitiful laughter.

Laboring with every breath, I yell to Father, "Crazy man! Shut your mouth. You and I are here because we deserve to be."

That is the last thing I said to Father. He doesn't say another word. He has laughed his last breath.

The intense heat of the sun beats on my naked torso. We have been hanging on these crosses for many hours now. The sun is high. It's hot and humid. No relief from a quick breeze passing by. It's miserable, and the pain reminds me I'm hanging in the sky only by rusty nails piercing through my hands and feet.

My mind rewinds. I see the many healings Jesus performed. There were many, so many, in fact, my father and I talked about how we couldn't keep up with writing them all down.

Those who couldn't see, now can. People I knew who had never walked in their life, got up and ran away, praising his name. Our childhood friend who was sick for eighteen years—he healed her. He changed Tabitha's life. She is a new person because of Jesus. I saw thousands have a meal with Jesus, fed with only two fish and five loathes of bread. No person should be able to walk on water, but Jesus did.

Then there is me. Jesus has been part of my life since we were boys. I have only allowed myself to know him as the kid down the street or the religious freak with the conviction of sharing the Good News with the lost. I never thought I could or should trust anybody. I have made my heart cold and hard since I can remember. And that's not all my father's fault either. I chose to be that person, but now, as I hang here, the bodily pain has been replaced with the heartfelt pain of not being the person I should have been. It's too late. I can never go back and change. I create a list of regrets in my mind: I will never be good enough. Never be forgiven or serve God. I'll never give enough to his ministry, help others in need, forgive myself. I'll never do enough to deserve God's love or do enough to be in the presence of the heavenly Father one day. No, I am beyond enough.

With my head bowed, I have an intense desire for the first time in my life to say a prayer. So, I do, softly. Not knowing what I'm doing really, the words simply flow from my heart to my lips. Immediately, my heart opens inside me. I feel the warmth of truth and belief run through my heart. It's no longer a cold, hardened, dead heart. It's alive for the first time in my life. I summon all the strength I have left and turn my head toward Jesus.

"Jesus! Jesus, are you still there, alive?"

"Yes, Seth, I am."

"Jesus, remember me when you come into your kingdom."

Jesus has to make the same painful effort to talk as I did. The effort takes his breath away, but he turns his face to me and, with a smile forcing its way past the blood, sweat, and spittle, says, "Truly I say to you, today my grace erases all your *enoughs*. I am . . . I am all you need. I am your enough. Today you shall be with me in paradise."

Without warning, the sky turns from the intense brightness of the noon sun to the darkest I have ever experienced. I see Jesus' body flinch as if it can't take anymore, that it will be over soon. With a loud strong voice, Jesus cries out, "My God . . . My God, why have you forsaken me?"

The ground shakes all around us as if in answer to his call. My cross sways in unison with the movement of the ground.

One of the guards runs up to Jesus and offers him a sponge dipped in wine. But Jesus refuses the drink. The earth moves restlessly as Jesus cries, "It is finished!"

Jesus is gone now. He's no longer breathing. People nearby are crying in mourning. One of the soldiers who was charged with guarding us threw down his shield and sword. "Truly this was the Son of God!" he shouts.

They run off, wasting no time getting off the hill. Straining every muscle, I have left, I look out into the crowd. Many are scurrying around like mice, looking for their next meal. A few newly healed people linger. Jesus' mother is sobbing, and one of the disciples is with her. I see my mother with Tabitha. Their arms are around each other.

My breathing is getting shorter, my lungs are harder to fill. But my eyes find and lock in with Tabitha's. Without my having to say a word, I know she knows. She knows that I now know the truth too, that I believe in Jesus, and that soon I will be with him and his heavenly Father in paradise.

But I am not ready to go yet. I have one more thing I want to do. As I turn my head to look at Father one last time. I say as if he can hear me, "Father, you were a hard man, causing me much physical and emotional pain, but you can't take away that moment we shared in the river that summer day. The time you fell headfirst into the river, then you pulled me in. We laughed and embraced, as fathers and sons sometimes do. I love you Father . . . and most of all, I forgive you."

My eyes go dim, the earth becomes silent, and my last breath leaves my body as the hand of Jesus reaches down and pulls me into his arms.

Chapter Forty-Five

Tabitha

That's it. He is gone. Seth's fight is over. He simply has no more breath to take. Seth's beaten and bruised face appears to be at peace, a peace he never believed possible for him. I believe Seth accepted Jesus as his Lord and Savior before he took his last breath. Believing that gives me joy and a sense of peace I will see him again someday.

I take Naomi and pull her close to me. We lean on each other, crying uncontrollably. The darkness settles over the hill, and cries of the crowd howl around us. Some are so upset they are bent over at the waist, trying to catch their breath as they become physically sick. Thankfully, many of the people who rallied for Jesus' torture and death have taken their celebrations far away.

A soldier lugs a large hammer made from wood and stone toward Aran. Without checking to make sure Aran is dead, the soldier swings the oversized hammer at Aran's legs and delivers a smashing blow.

I was never a fan of Aran, but I shield Naomi from the horrific sight of her husband's legs being shattered. The only pain I feel is from the harsh way the soldiers are treating Aran. As the soldier walks away, two other guards approach Aran and take him off the cross.

The first soldier lifts his hammer again and walks toward Jesus. A second stands in between the crosses of Jesus and

Seth. The second guard raises his hand to the hammer bearer as if to say hold on. The two Romans walk over to Jesus and Seth and inspect their bodies, touching their wrists and rib cages. The guards chat for a second.

Then the second guard lugs his hammer toward Seth. Realizing what is coming next, I bury Naomi's head in my chest, covering her ears. The guard raises the hammer, and takes his swing, breaking Seth's right leg. A second swing smashes the left.

Then he shrugs and leans the thick handle against his shoulder. He walks away looking disappointed Jesus is already dead and there can be no more pain inflicted.

I feel myself breathing again. He's not going to break any more legs today.

The remaining soldier motions for another soldier to come to him. I know what for. They are going to take Seth down off the cross. I turn Naomi away, so we don't watch. If they aren't respectful, we don't need to witness any more abuse on Seth.

After the Romans take Seth and Aran off their crosses, a well-dressed man and two others—none of them soldiers—begin the process of taking down Jesus' body from his cross. They position the same ladder used earlier to place the sign above Jesus' head. One man holds the ladder as the other climbs it. After pulling out each nail as gingerly as possible, they wrap him in linen and head down the hill. Jesus' mother and several other women follow.

It appears that Jesus has a burial place and a caretaker. But I don't know what will happen to Seth's and Aran's bodies. Naomi can't possibly take them back to Nazareth. She has no money to pay for a proper burial here either. I manage to get one soldier's attention.

"Woman, what do you want?" he asks.

"Sir, can you please tell me what will happen to their bodies? Do you know where they will be taken? Their family has no funds for a proper burial."

"Their bodies will be buried in the Potter's Field, the place for nobodies. They won't even get a headstone. I guess they'll get what they deserve."

The soldier laughs, turns around, and walks away. An ox pulling a wagon tops the hill. The soldiers pick up Seth and Aran and toss them over the side of the wagon and onto a thin pile of straw. They throw them just as they would a sack of garbage. I try my best to be strong for Naomi but the soldiers' disrespect for the dead is almost more than I can take.

But I gather my composer and gently help Naomi stand. The wind blows a piece of linen toward me. It's left over from the men who took Jesus' body. Just as the ox starts to walk off with Seth's and Aran's bodies, I yell, "Stop! Please hold on for a moment."

The soldier leading the ox looks no older than fifteen. He stops as if he is obeying the cry of a mother, his mother. I walk Naomi over to the back of the wagon, and together we stretch the piece of linen and place it over Seth's and Aran's bodies. Tears stream down our cheeks.

The young soldier says, "I'm sorry, but we must go now."

The boy does all he can to appear a strong warrior. He fights back the tears falling off his face as he struggles to make the ox obey his commands. The wagon heads down the hill, and we follow.

Chapter Forty-Six

Tabitha

"It's empty, Naomi."

My words draw Naomi out of the small room we temporarily share in her brother Benjamin's house. We have been here since the beginning of the end. From conviction to crucifixion.

Benjamin was most consoling when it came to Seth. Aran, he refused to acknowledge. I heard him tell Naomi more than once in our short stay, "You should have left him a long time ago. Brought Seth here. Stayed with us."

Naomi would just listen to her brother and nod her head to confirm what Benjamin was telling her. My heart broke over and over for her.

"What's empty?" Naomi asks, walking into the main living area.

I point to the water jug on the floor. "That. I need to go get some water. Do you want to come with me? Maybe a walk and some fresh air will do us both good and clear our minds. We have been cooped up in your brother's house since Friday. It's going on three days."

"Oh, Tabitha, I don't feel up to a walk right now. You go."

I kick her sandals closer to her. Reaching out my hand I grab her wrist and throw a shawl around her neck.

"I will not take no for an answer. Please, I don't want to

go by myself. Remember the time I went and got water and met Jesus? It changed my life."

"If it will shut you up, okay." We both had a smile and light laughter.

I keep hold of Naomi and lead her out the door and down the path that passes the Fish Gate.

Naomi and I walk quietly. I soak in the warmth of the sunshine, hoping it will heal my broken heart.

All of a sudden, a woman comes barreling around a brush-covered corner of the road. She nearly knocks Naomi and me into the next village.

I manage to stay on my feet. Naomi is not so lucky. She looks embarrassed as she frantically tries to get back up while searching for her left sandal.

I recognize the woman as Mary Magdalene. She reaches down to Naomi to help her up.

"Oh, I'm so sorry," Mary Magdalene says. "Please, take my hand. I didn't mean to run over you two like this. But you won't believe what I just saw."

"Believe what?" I say as I dump dirt from the missing sandal and hand it back to Naomi.

"The large stone that sealed the tomb has been rolled back."

"Which tomb are you talking about?"

"Jesus' tomb! Mary Magdalene raises her hands to the sky like everyone should know what she means. "The stone was rolled away."

"Are you sure it was the tomb used for Jesus' body?"

Mary Magdalene sighs in exasperation. "Yes, of course. I helped prepare the tomb for him. I watched as they put Jesus' body inside. I saw the effort the men took to seal that tomb. No one was going to get in there. I know what I know. Not only has the rock sealing the tomb been moved, but Jesus wasn't in there when I looked inside. The tomb was empty."

Mary grabs my arms just above my elbows and shakes

me gently. She says again, "It's empty. Jesus is not in there."

Naomi is now back on her feet. "Do you think grave robbers stole Jesus' body?"

Mary Magdalene lets go of my arms. She answers, "Well, at first, I thought that too. I just stood there crying. Then a voice from inside the tomb spoke to me. 'Woman, why are you crying?'

"Startled, I said, 'I am crying because they have taken away Jesus, and I don't know where they put him.'

"Then another voice said to me, 'Woman, why are you weeping? Whom are you seeking?'

I am stunned. Mary Magdalene's story is impossible. But then I remember Jesus regularly proved the impossible was possible. "Two people?" I ask. "Who were they?"

Mary Magdalene explains, "I just assumed the man speaking was the caretaker of the tomb. So, I said, 'Sir, if you have laid him somewhere else just tell me where and I will take him away.'

"Then a man behind me says, 'Mary! Stop clinging to me, for I have not yet ascended to the Father. Go to my disciples and say to them that I will ascend to my Father and your Father, and My God and your God.'

"I turned and cried out, 'My teacher!'

Mary Magdalene puts her hands on her hips. She seems defensive but also elated. "I saw him," she says. "Jesus is alive! That's when I took off running as fast as I could. I am on my way to tell his disciples what just happened."

I look at Naomi. She seems to be in shock.

"Mary, do you know where the disciples are?" I ask.

"Yes, they're staying at a house owned by one of Jesus' friends. It's on this path, not too far from here." She waves. "I must go now."

I look at Naomi and then back at Mary. "Can we come with you?"

"Sure," Mary says. "Follow me."

Naomi takes hold of my arm so tight it's close to hurting.

"Tabitha, wait," she says. "Are you sure what this woman told us is possible? We saw with our own eyes that Jesus died on the cross. It was just this past Friday, barely three days ago. How can he be alive? Perhaps it's one of his followers pretending to be him. I think you just need to accept the fact that Jesus is gone. This fantasy isn't healthy."

"Three days ago? Three days? *Three?* Naomi, don't you remember?"

"Remember what?"

"Jesus said more than once, 'Destroy this temple, and in three days I will raise it up.' Jesus wasn't talking about rebuilding the stone temple. No, the temple is his *body*. Three days ago, they destroyed Jesus—the temple—on the cross. But today, the tomb is empty. Not because someone took his body. You can't take something that's not there to take. Jesus is not there because he is alive. Not a stone or a tomb can hold Jesus in the ground. That's it! He's the holy temple he was always talking about. He has risen!"

I nod. "So yes, Naomi, I do believe that Mary saw our risen Lord. We must go with her to be with his disciples."

Turning back to Mary, I feel my heart is healing now. It's been given a new life. I say, "Mary let's go. We will follow you to the house."

Mary Magdalene takes off down the path. Barely keeping up with her, Naomi and I make it to the house.

We find a place in the back of the room, and I press myself against the wall. Naomi slips her hand into mine.

A man somewhere in front says, "Unless I can see and touch where the nails entered his body, I will not believe it is him."

Another voice near him says, "Thomas, reach here with your finger and touch and feel my hands. Do not be an unbeliever, but a believer."

I move to the left to see around the crowd. The man called Thomas places his hand on the second man's palm. With a quavering voice, Thomas says, "My Lord and my

God!

With people standing all around us, it is a challenge to see clearly who the second voice belongs to. I begin to think, hope, and want so much for this to be Jesus. The unknown speaker goes on.

"Go into all the world and preach the gospel to all creation. It is written that the Christ would suffer and rise again from the dead on the third day."

I immediately look over to Naomi and squeeze her hand.

The man continues preaching. "And that repentance for forgiveness of sins will be proclaimed in God's name to all the nations, beginning from Jerusalem. You are witnesses of these things. Go therefore and make disciples of all nations, baptizing them in the name of the Father and the Son and the Holy Spirit. Teach them to observe all that I commanded you. Lo, I am with you always, even to the end of age."

I close my eyes and listen. My mind goes back to the times I heard Jesus speak. I remember that he wanted to be my well of never-ending water of life. I see him in my mind's eye healing many with his simple command, and then at the end nailed to a cross, crying out to his Father, "God forgive them for they know not what they do."

My eyes open wide. The person in front of me shifts, and then I see him as clearly as I have seen anything before.

I know who that man is! It's Jesus! Jesus is here. He has risen! He is alive! I feel a sense of love and grace emanating from Jesus that can't be explained.

I release Naomi's hand, putting my arm around her neck I lean toward her. "It's him," I say. "It's Jesus. He is alive."

Naomi wipes the tears from her eyes. She looks up at me and says, "Yes, our Lord and Savior is alive."

Naomi and I continue to embrace, listening as Jesus tells us about the way to have everlasting life through him.

I want so much to know if Seth accepted Jesus Christ as his Lord and Savior. As my mind searches deep for the answer, Jesus says, "Peace be with you."

He lifts his hands, and as he says a blessing over the room, the ceiling turns to a bright blue sky as his body begins to float. Higher and higher he rises toward the heavens. My mind isn't playing tricks on me. No, this is real. Everyone is on their feet. Singing and shouting praises to him. Naomi shouts out, praising God. The disciples are also shouting praises to God.

It is a grand time of worship. The worship is not about my needs and my healing. No, I want my worship to be all about God.

We are all witnessing the same thing. I am not able to take my eyes off Jesus. I see him being received into heaven. It is so amazingly beautiful. I see unimaginable colors. I have never seen colors like these before. I see two waterfalls. The luster of the water is like nothing on earth. They don't seem to have a beginning or end, but a flow continuously. Between the waterfalls, I see what looks like people in white robes. Some are waving palm branches, some are wearing crowns with the most spectacular jewels, sapphires, and other stones I can't describe. All are worshiping God.

I am filled with overflowing joy when I see Jesus sitting at the right hand of his Father, God. And behind them stands Seth.

Author's Reflections:

Seth almost ran out of time. Time to accept Jesus as his Lord and Savior. But with a breath or two left, he said yes to Jesus. Yes, to Jesus' gift of salvation.

That is what grace is all about. Not having a ''to do'' list of things you must complete to earn salvation. That was given by Jesus on the cross next to him. Jesus carried all our sins on that cross that day, so we didn't have to.

Not having to earn it, I believe if Seth could have come down off that cross after saying yes to Jesus, he would be shouting Jesus' praises to the mountain tops. Seth would have been the first one in worship service on the sabbath with his hands raised high in the air. He would have wanted to give tithes and offerings not as an obligation, but as a blessing returned to Jesus. He would have run as fast as he could to the closest watering hole to be baptized. Not because he has to, but because he wants to.

Seth couldn't, and neither can we do enough to earn Jesus' salvation. It's a gift, a gift of grace available to all who say yes, who ask Jesus to remember them in paradise.

If you enjoyed Seth's Cross, but are a little sad that he died at the end, stay tuned, it's not the end of his story.

Invitation:

If your heart's desire is to spend eternity in heaven with Jesus, that gift of God's grace is available to you.

Simply pray,

"Lord Jesus, I come to you now, admitting I am a sinner, asking for your forgiveness. I believe with all my heart that you died on the cross for my sins and rose again. Please come into my heart and be my Lord and Savior. Thank you for your grace and for giving me eternal life. Amen."

Wow! If you prayed that pray all in heaven are singing and dancing rejoicing your decision.

Seek to serve Jesus and others as Seth would have if you could have come off that cross. Read the Bible, seek others who are believers, and pray to Jesus often as his word instructs us in 1 Thessalonians 5:16-18

"Rejoice always, pray continually…"

ABOUT THE AUTHOR

Author Jeff Randall knows firsthand the power of God's grace. His journey hasn't been perfect, but through every misstep, he has learned that grace isn't earned—it's a gift. Randall's message is clear: "You are redeemable. Say yes to Jesus by remembering the conversation on the cross."

He is honored to share this truth in Seth's Cross and is deeply grateful for the path God has allowed for his life along with his wife, their two sons, two daughters-in-law, and two beautiful granddaughters.

Join Jeff in the pages of Seth's Cross and explore the power of choices, redemption, and the limitless grace of God.